CW01011147

The Young Oxford Book of War Stories

Other books by James Riordan

The Young Oxford Book of Football Stories
The Young Oxford Book of Sports Stories

Korean Folk-tales
Russian Folk-tales
Pinocchio
Gulliver's Travels
King Arthur
The Wizard of Oz
Sweet Clarinet
The Prisoner
When the Guns Fall Silent

The Young Oxford Book of

War Stories

James Riordan

'If evil people can get together to make war, why cannot the good people of the world, who are infinitely more numerous, come together to make peace?'

Leo Tolstoy, *War and Peace*

For Nathalie, Bruce, and Imogen
May you never know war

OXFORD
UNIVERSITY PRESS

Great Clarendon Street, Oxford OX2 6DP

Oxford University Press is a department of the University of Oxford.
It furthers the University's objective of excellence in research, scholarship,
and education by publishing worldwide in

Oxford New York
Athens Auckland Bangkok Bogotá Buenos Aires Calcutta
Cape Town Chennai Dar es Salaam Delhi Florence Hong Kong Istanbul
Karachi Kuala Lumpur Madrid Melbourne Mexico City Mumbai
Nairobi Paris São Paulo Shanghai Singapore Taipei Tokyo Toronto Warsaw

and associated companies in Berlin Ibadan

First published 2001

British Library Cataloguing in Publication Data available

ISBN 0 19 278174 X (hardback)
ISBN 0 19 278175 8 (paperback)

1 3 5 7 9 10 8 6 4 2

Typeset by AFS Image Setters Ltd, Glasgow

Printed in Great Britain
by Biddles Ltd, Guildford and King's Lynn

Contents

Introduction

Whom shall we blame for the folly of war?
Whom shall we tell these stories for?
Who will believe
The sadness of death,
The terror, the fear, and the emptiness—
What can they know
Of the vacant eyes
The sorrow too deep
In the heart that dies?

from 'Bomb Incident' by Barbara Catherine Edwards

War makes rattling good stories, as Thomas Hardy once said. Our selection of stories and poems has been chosen not only because their authors write entertaining yarns and moving verse. Most have seen war, heard it, smelt it; some, like Anne Frank and Wilfred Owen, died in it. So their accounts contain the whiff of gunsmoke, the stain of blood, the tragedy of death.

Out of the hundreds of wars that raged throughout the twentieth century, the three covered in this book were the longest and bloodiest. In total they lasted twenty years, a fifth of the century, and killed nearly 100 million people.

A hundred million people!

Shot, bayoneted, gassed, blown up, burnt, hacked to death.

The First World War lasted four years and claimed ten million lives.

The Second World War lasted six years and claimed over eighty million lives.

The Vietnam War lasted ten years, claiming three million lives and destroying half of Vietnam.

The writers are friend and foe—British and German, Russian and American. The first story is from

All Quiet on the Western Front by the German Erich Maria Remarque, perhaps the most remarkable and moving war novel ever written. Others—Russian, German, and English—convey in verse and prose the tragedy and utter waste of the 'Great War'.

The five British children's authors (though Anne Holm is actually Danish) write about World War II—Robert Westall and Robert Swindells on the 'home' war, Michael Morpurgo about a 'war horse', and Ian Serraillier and Anne Holm on refugees in occupied Europe.

The Dutch Anne Frank describes the plight of the Jews under the Nazis, while the Russian stories illustrate the tragedy of the nation that suffered worst in the war and contributed most to Hitler's defeat.

Since 1945, the end of World War II, no one has suffered as much as the people of Vietnam, invaded by the French, and then by the Americans. They provide proof that, if the cause is just, the poor and weak can overcome the rich and strong.

In her moving story, Rachel Anderson shows not only a nation's suffering, but how war can brutalize soldiers, turn men into beasts.

Finally, the women's poems on the two world wars are evidence enough that war is a woman's affair as well as a man's.

Above the roar of battle, one voice rises from all our stories. Its message is that war is not about glory, about dying nobly for one's country. It is about terror, stark terror, about a human being either waiting for death or trying desperately to avoid it, even if that means killing a complete stranger, losing all human dignity and feelings.

This is best expressed by Wilfred Owen (who was killed one week before the end of World War I), in his poem 'Dulce et Decorum est' which you will find on page 114.

James Riordan

To Posterity

You that will emerge from the deluge
In which we drowned,
When you speak of our shortcomings
Remember too
The bleak age
Which you have escaped.

For, changing countries more often than shoes, we
walked
Through the wars of the classes, despairing
When there was injustice only and no rebellion.

And yet we know well:
Even hatred of vileness
Distorts a man's features.
Even anger at injustice
Makes hoarse his voice. Ah, we
Who desired to prepare the soil for kindness
Could not ourselves be kind.

But you, when the times permit
Men to be the helpers of men
Remember us
With indulgence.

Bertolt Brecht

Bertolt Brecht (1898–1956), author of *Mother Courage* and *The Threepenny Opera*, was a medical orderly in World War I.

from *All Quiet on the Western Front*

ERICH MARIA REMARQUE

Erich Maria Remarque was born in Osnabrück, northern Germany, in 1898. So he was sixteen when the First World War broke out. He was called up in November 1916, sent to the Front in June 1917, and wounded by a British shell during the battle known as Passchendaele in July–August 1917. That ended his war action.

He published his first major novel in 1929 as *Im Westen nichts Neues* (*Nothing New on the Western Front*) which became an instant success—one of the greatest war novels ever written. But when the Nazis came to power in 1933, they burned his books, claiming that *All Quiet on the Western Front* was a betrayal of the German soldier. Remarque went to Switzerland and then, in 1939, to the United States. In 1948 he returned to Switzerland, dying there in 1970.

The book shows the war through the eyes of nineteen-year-old Paul Baümer. There are few military details, no heroics; the real enemy is death—though the word 'enemy' is rare. Baümer refers only to 'the others' or 'those over there'.

Every day and every hour, every shell and every dead man wear down our weak hold on life, and the years grind it down rapidly. I can see how it is already giving way around me.

Take the stupid business with Detering.

He was one of those who keep themselves very much to themselves. The unlucky thing for him was seeing a cherry tree in someone's garden. We had just come back from the front, and this cherry tree was suddenly there in front of us in the early morning light, just as we came around a bend in the road near our new quarters. It didn't have any leaves, but it was a single mass of white blossoms.

That evening Detering was nowhere to be found. Eventually he turned up, and he had a few twigs with cherry blossom in his hand. We had a laugh, and asked him if he was going courting. He didn't answer, and just lay down on his bed. That night I heard him moving about, and he seemed to be packing his things. I thought there might be trouble brewing, and went over to him. He acted as if nothing was the matter, and I said to him, 'Don't do anything daft, Detering.'

''Course not—I just can't get to sleep—'

'Why did you pick the cherry blossom?'

'I can pick cherry blossom if I want, can't I?' he said sullenly—and then he added after a while, 'I've got a big orchard with cherry trees back home. From the hayloft they look like one huge bed-sheet when they are in blossom, that's how white they are. It's at this time of the year.'

'Maybe you'll get leave. You might even be demobbed and sent home because you are a farmer.'

He nods, but his mind is elsewhere. When country

people like him get into a state they have a peculiar expression on their faces, a bit bovine, but also with an almost luminous look of yearning, half idiocy and half rapture. To try and get him out of himself I ask him for a chunk of bread. He gives it to me without question. That's suspicious, because he is usually pretty stingy. So I keep an eye on him. Nothing happens, and in the morning he is his usual self.

He had probably realized that I was watching him. Two mornings later, and he is missing after all. I notice, but keep quiet about it so as to give him a bit of time—perhaps he'll make it. A few men have got through to Holland.

But at roll call his absence is spotted. A week later we hear that the military police, or rather the special battle police everyone hates, have picked him up. He was heading for Germany—that was obviously completely hopeless, and it was equally obvious that everything else he had done was simply stupid. Anyone could have worked out that he had only deserted out of homesickness and a momentary aberration. But what does a court martial miles behind the lines know about things like that? Nothing more's been heard of Detering.

But they break through in other ways as well, those dangerously dammed-up feelings—like steam escaping from an over-heated boiler. It's worth reporting how Berger met his end, for example.

Our trenches have long since been shot to pieces, and the front is so fluid that trench warfare is not really possible any more. Once an attack and a counter-attack have come and gone, all that remains is a ragged line and a bitter struggle from one bomb crater to the next. The front line has been broken, and little groups have

dug themselves in everywhere, fighting from clusters of foxholes.

We are in one shell hole, with English troops already on one side of us—they are turning our flank and getting round behind us. We are surrounded. It is not easy to surrender. There is fog and smoke all around, and nobody would realize that we were trying to give ourselves up, and perhaps we don't even want to—no one is quite sure in times like this.

We can hear the explosions of hand-grenades getting closer. Our machine-gun sweeps the sector in front of us. The water in the cooling system evaporates and we pass the container round quickly—everyone pisses into it and we have water again and can go on firing. But behind us the explosions are getting closer. In a few minutes we'll be done for.

Suddenly another machine-gun starts up from very close by. It is in a crater near us, and Berger has got hold of it; now there is a counter-attack from behind, we get out and manage to move backwards and join up with the rest.

Afterwards, by the time we have found some decent cover, one of the food carriers tells us that there is a wounded messenger dog a couple of hundred yards away.

'Where?' asks Berger.

The food carrier describes the place for him. Berger sets off to fetch the animal or to shoot it. Even six months ago he would not have bothered about it, and would have behaved sensibly. We try to stop him. But when he sets off—and he's serious about it—all we can say is 'He's crazy', and let him go. These front-line breakdowns can be dangerous if you can't wrestle the man to the ground straight away and hold him there. And Berger is over six foot and the strongest man in the company.

He really is mad, because he has to go through the barrage—but that sudden bolt from the blue that hovers over every one of us has hit him, and now he is a man possessed. The way it takes other people is to make them scream with rage, or run away, and there was one man who just kept on trying to dig himself into the earth with his hands, his feet, and his mouth.

Of course there is a lot of shamming in situations like this, but even the shamming is really a symptom as well. Berger tries to put the dog out of its misery and is carried back with a shot through the pelvis, and even one of the men who fetches him gets a bullet wound in the calf.

Müller is dead. He got a Very light in the stomach from close to. He lived for another half-hour, fully conscious and in terrible agony. Before he died he gave me his paybook and passed on his boots—the ones he inherited from Kemmerich that time. I wear them, because they are a good fit. Tjaden will get them after me—I've promised him.

We were actually able to bury Müller, but he probably won't rest in peace for long. Our lines are being moved back. There are too many fresh British and American regiments over there. There is too much corned beef and white flour. And too many new guns. Too many aircraft.

But we are thin and starving. Our food is so bad and full of so much ersatz stuff that it makes us ill. The factory owners in Germany have grown rich, while dysentery racks our guts. The latrine poles always have men squatting over them. The people at home ought to be shown these grey or yellow, wretched, beaten-down faces, these figures who are bent double because of the

enteritis that is squeezing the blood out of their bodies so much that the best they can do is to grin through lips trembling with pain, and say 'It's hardly worth pulling your trousers up again.'

Our artillery can't really do much—they have too little ammunition, and the gun-barrels are so clapped out that they can't shoot straight, and scatter stuff over towards us. We haven't enough horses. Our new drafts are pitiful lads who really need a rest, unable to carry a pack but able to die. In their thousands. They understand nothing of the war, they just go over the top and allow themselves to be shot down. One single airman knocks off two whole companies of them just for fun, when they were just off a troop train and had no idea about taking cover.

'Germany must be nearly empty,' says Kat.

We are quite without hope that there could ever be an end to this. We can't think nearly so far ahead. You might stop a bullet and be killed; you might be wounded, and then the next stop is the military hospital. As long as they haven't amputated anything, sooner or later you'll fall into the hands of one of those staff doctors with a war service ribbon on his chest who says, 'What's this? One leg a bit on the short side? You won't need to run at the front if you've got any guts. Passed fit for service! Dismiss!'

Kat tells a story that has done the rounds all along the front, from Flanders to the Vosges, about the staff doctor who reads out the names of the men who come up for medical inspection, and, when the man appears, doesn't even look up, but says, 'Passed fit for service, we need soldiers at the front.' A man with a wooden leg comes up before him, the doctor passes him fit for service again—'And then,' Kat raises his voice, 'the man says to him, "I've already got a wooden leg; but if

I go up the line now and they shoot my head off, I'll have a wooden head made, and then I'll become a staff doctor."' We all think that's a really good one.

There may be good doctors—many of them are; but with the hundreds of examinations he has, every soldier will at some time or other get into the clutches of one of the hero-makers, and there are lots of them, whose aim is to turn as many of those on their lists who have only been passed for work detail or garrison duty into class A1, fit for active service.

There are plenty of stories like that, and most of them are more bitter. But for all that, they have nothing to do with mutiny or malingering; they are honest, and they call a spade a spade; because there really *is* a lot of fraud, injustice, and petty nastiness in the army. But isn't it enough that regiment after regiment goes off into a fight which is becoming increasingly pointless in spite of everything, and that attack after attack is launched, even though our line is retreating and crumbling?

Tanks, which used to be objects of ridicule, have become a major weapon. They come rolling forward in a long line, heavily armoured, and they embody the horror of war for us more than anything else.

We cannot see the gun batteries that are bombarding us, and the oncoming waves of enemy attackers are human beings just like we are—but tanks are machines, and their caterpillar tracks run on as endlessly as the war itself. They spell out annihilation when they roll without feeling into the shell holes and then climb out again, inexorably, a fleet of roaring, fire-spitting ironclads, invulnerable steel beasts that crush the dead and the wounded. Before these we shrivel down into our thin skins, in the face of their colossal force our arms are like straws and our hand-grenades are like matches.

Shells, gas clouds, and flotillas of tanks—crushing, devouring, death.

Dysentery, influenza, typhus—choking, scalding, death.

Trench, hospital, mass grave—there are no other possibilities.

In one attack Bertinck, our company commander, is killed. He was one of those fine front-line officers who are always at the forefront of every tricky situation. He had been with us for two years without being wounded, so something had to happen in the end. We are sitting in a shell hole and we have been surrounded. With the smell of cordite, the smell of oil or petrol wafts across to us. Two men with a flame-thrower are spotted, one with the cylinder on his back, the other holding the pipe where the fire shoots out. If they get close enough to reach us, we've had it, because just at the moment we can't get back.

We start to fire at them. But they work their way closer to us, and things look bad. Bertinck is with us in the hole. When he sees that we are not hitting them because the firing is so heavy and we have to concentrate too much on cover, he takes a rifle, crawls out of the hole and aims, lying there propped on his elbows. He shoots—and at the same moment a bullet smacks down by him with a crack, he has been hit. But he stays where he is and aims again—he lowers his rifle once, and then takes aim; at last the shot rings out. Bertinck drops the gun, says, 'Good' and slides back. The second man with the flame-thrower is wounded and falls, the pipe is wrenched out of the other one's hands, fire is sprayed all around and the man is burning.

Bertinck has been hit in the chest. A short while later a piece of shrapnel smashes away the lower part of his face. That same piece of shrapnel has enough force left to rip open Leer's side. Leer groans and props himself on his arms, but he bleeds to death very quickly and no one can help him. After a few minutes he sinks down like a rubber tyre when the air escapes. What use is it to him now that he was so good at mathematics at school?

The months drag on. This summer of 1918 is the bloodiest and the hardest. The days are like angels in blue and gold, rising up untouchable above the circle of destruction. Everyone knows that we are losing the war. Nobody talks about it much. We are retreating. We won't be able to attack again after this massive offensive. We have no more men and no more ammunition.

But the campaign goes on—the dying continues.

Summer, 1918. Never has life in its simplest outline seemed so desirable to us as it does now; the poppies in the fields near our base camp, the shiny beetles on the blades of grass, the warm evenings in the cool, half-dark rooms, black, mysterious trees at twilight, the stars and the streams, dreams and the long sleep. Oh life, life, life!

Summer, 1918. Never has more been suffered in silence as in the moment when we set off for the front. The wild and urgent rumours of an armistice and peace have surfaced again, they disturb the heart and make setting out harder than ever.

Summer, 1918. Never has life at the front been more bitter and more full of horror than when we are under fire, when the pallid faces are pressed into the mud and

the fists are clenched and your whole being is saying, No! No! No, not now! Not now at the very last minute!

Summer, 1918. A wind of hope sweeping over the burnt-out fields, a raging fever of impatience, of disappointment, the most agonizing terror of death, the impossible question: why? Why don't they stop? And why are there all these rumours about it ending?

There are so many airmen here, and they are so skilful that they can hunt down individuals like rabbits. For every German aircraft there are five British or American ones. For every hungry, tired German soldier in the trenches there are five strong, fresh men on the enemy side. For every German army-issue loaf there are fifty cans of beef over there. We haven't been defeated, because as soldiers we are better and more experienced; we have simply been crushed and pushed back by forces many times superior to ours.

Several weeks of steady rain lie behind us—grey skies, grey, liquid earth, grey death. When we go out the damp penetrates right through our coats and uniforms—and it is like that all the time we are at the front. We can never get dry. Anyone who still has a pair of boots ties them up at the top with little bags of sand to stop the muddy water getting in so quickly. Rifles are caked in mud, uniforms are caked in mud, everything is fluid and liquefied, a dripping, damp and oily mass of earth in which there are yellow puddles with spiral pools of blood, and in which the dead, the wounded, and the living are slowly swallowed up.

The storm is like a whiplash over us, the hail of shrapnel wrenches the sharp, children's cries of the wounded from the confusion of grey and yellow, and in

the night shattered life groans itself painfully into silence.

Our hands are earth, our bodies mud, and our eyes puddles of rain. We no longer know whether we are still alive or not.

Then heat steals into our shell holes, damp and oppressive, like a jellyfish, and on one of these late summer days, Kat topples over. I am alone with him. I bandage the wound. His shin seems to be shattered. Damage to the bone, and Kat groans in despair. 'Now of all times! Why did it have to be now . . . ?'

I comfort him. 'Who knows how much longer the whole mess will go on. At least you're out of it . . . '

The wound begins to bleed a lot. Kat cannot stay where he is while I try and find a stretcher. I don't know where the nearest casualty post is, either.

Kat is not very heavy; so I take him on my back and carry him to the rear, to the dressing station.

Twice we stop to rest. Being carried is causing him a lot of pain. We don't talk much. I've undone the neck of my tunic and I'm breathing heavily and sweating, and my face is red from the effort of carrying him. In spite of that I make us move on, because the terrain is dangerous.

'All right to move, Kat?'

'I'll have to be, Paul.'

'Let's go.'

I help him up. He stands on his good leg and steadies himself against a tree. Then I get hold of his wounded leg very carefully, he pushes upwards, and I get my arm under the knee of his good leg.

Moving becomes more difficult. Often, shells whistle past. I go as fast as I can, because the blood from his wounded leg is dripping on to the ground. We can't

really protect ourselves from shell-blast, because it is over before we could have taken cover.

We get down in a small shell crater until it quietens down a bit. I give Kat some tea from my flask. We smoke a cigarette. 'Yes, Kat,' I say sadly, 'we'll get split up now after all.'

He says nothing, and just looks at me.

'Kat, do you still remember how we bagged that goose? And how you got me out of the scrap when I was still a raw recruit and I'd just been wounded for the first time? I cried, then, Kat, and it was nearly three years ago.'

Kat nods.

The fear of loneliness wells up in me. If Kat is taken out I'll have no friends here at all.

'Kat, we must get in touch again, if peace really does come before you get back.'

'With what's happened to the old leg, do you reckon I'll ever be fit for service again?' he asks bitterly.

'You'll be able to convalesce in peace and quiet. The joint is still OK. Maybe it will all be all right.'

'Give me another cigarette,' he says.

'Maybe we could do something or other together afterwards, Kat.' I am very sad, it is impossible that Kat, my friend Kat, Kat with the drooping shoulders and the thin, soft moustache, Kat, whom I know in a different way from every other person, Kat, the man I have shared these years with—it is impossible that I might never see Kat again.

'Give me your address anyway, Kat. Here's mine, I'll write it down for you.'

I tuck the piece of paper into the breast-pocket of my tunic. I feel so isolated already, even though he is still sitting there with me. Maybe I should shoot myself in the foot, just so that I can stay with him?

Suddenly Kat makes a choking noise and goes greenish-yellow. 'We'd better move,' he stammers.

I jump up, eager to help him. I hoist him up and set off with long, slow strides so as not to shake his leg too much.

My throat is parched and I have red and black spots before my eyes by the time I eventually stumble, doggedly and relentlessly, into the casualty station.

There I drop to my knees, but I have enough strength left to fall on to the side where Kat's good leg is. After a few minutes I ease myself up slowly. My legs and my hands are still shaking violently, and I have trouble finding my flask to take a drink out of it. My lips tremble as I do so. But Kat is safe.

After a time I am able to distinguish sounds from the barrage of noise battering in my ears.

'You could have saved yourself the trouble,' says an orderly.

I stare at him, uncomprehending.

He points to Kat. 'He's dead.'

I can't understand what he means. 'He's got a lower leg wound,' I say.

The orderly stops. 'Yes, that as well . . .'

I turn round. My eyes are still dimmed, I have started to sweat again and it is running into my eyes. I wipe it away and look at Kat. He is lying still. 'Must have fainted,' I say quickly.

The orderly whistles softly. 'I know more about it than you do. He's dead. I'll bet you anything.'

I shake my head. 'Can't be. I was talking to him not ten minutes ago. He's fainted.'

Kat's hands are warm. I get hold of his shoulders to give him some tea to bring him round. Then I feel how my fingers are getting wet. When I take my hands out

from behind his head they are bloody. The orderly whistles between his teeth. 'Told you so—'

Without my noticing it, Kat got a splinter of shrapnel in the head on the way. It's only a little hole. It must have been a tiny, stray fragment. But it was enough. Kat is dead.

I stand up slowly.

'Do you want to take his paybook and his things?' the orderly asks me.

I nod and he gives them to me.

The orderly is baffled. 'You're not related, are you?'

No, we are not related.

Am I walking? Do I still have legs? I look up, I look about me. And then I turn right round, and then I stop. Everything is just the same as usual. It's only that Private Stanislaus Katczinsky is dead.

After that I remember nothing.

It's autumn. There are not many of the old lot left. I am the last one of the seven from our class still here.

Everyone is talking about peace or an armistice. Everyone is waiting. If there is another disappointment, they will collapse, the hopes are too strong, they can no longer be pushed aside without exploding. If there is no peace, then there will be a revolution.

I have been given fourteen days' rest because I swallowed a bit of gas. I sit all day in a little garden in the sunshine. There will soon be an armistice, I believe in it too, now. Then we shall go home.

My thoughts stop there and I can't push them on any further. What attract me so strongly and await me are raw feelings—lust for life, desire for home, the blood itself, the intoxication of escaping. But these aren't exactly goals.

If we had come back in 1916 we could have unleashed a storm out of the pain and intensity of our experiences. If we go back now we shall be weary, broken-down, burnt-out, rootless and devoid of hope. We shall no longer be able to cope.

No one will understand us—because in front of us there is a generation of men who did, it is true, share the years out here with us, but who already had a bed and a job and who are going back to their old positions, where they will forget all about the war—and behind us, a new generation is growing up, one like we used to be, and that generation will be strangers to us and will push us aside. We are superfluous even to ourselves, we shall grow older, a few will adapt, others will make adjustments, and many of us will not know what to do—the years will trickle away, and eventually we shall perish.

But perhaps all these thoughts of mine are just melancholy and confusion, which will be blown away like dust when I am standing underneath the poplars once again, and listening to the rustle of their leaves. It cannot have vanished entirely, that tenderness that troubles our blood, the uncertainty, the worry, all the things to come, the thousand faces of the future, the music of dreams and books, the rustling and the idea of women. All this cannot have collapsed in the shelling, the despair, and the army brothels.

The trees here glow bright and gold, the rowan berries are red against the leaves, white country roads run on towards the horizon, and the canteens are all buzzing like beehives with rumours of peace.

I stand up.

I am very calm. Let the months come, and the years, they'll take nothing more from me, they *can* take nothing more from me. I am so alone and so devoid of

any hope that I can confront them without fear. Life, which carried me through these years, is still there in my hands and in my eyes. Whether or not I have mastered it, I do not know. But as long as life is there it will make its own way, whether my conscious self likes it or not.

* * *

He fell in October 1918, on a day that was so still and quiet along the entire front line that the army despatches restricted themselves to the single sentence: that there was nothing new to report on the western front.

He had sunk forwards and was lying on the ground as if asleep. When they turned him over, you could see that he could not have suffered long—his face wore an expression that was so composed that it looked as if he were almost happy that it had turned out that way.

Battlefield

Yielding clod lulls iron off to sleep
bloods clot the patches where they oozed
rusts crumble
fleshes slime
sucking lusts around decay.
Murder on murder
blinks
in childish eyes.

August Stramm

August Stramm (1874–1915) was killed in action on the Eastern Front in the first year of war.

from *The Silver Sword*

IAN SERRAILLIER

This is the story of a Polish family, and of what happened to them during the Second World War and immediately afterwards. Their home was in a suburb of Warsaw where the father, Joseph Balicki, was headmaster of a primary school. He and his Swiss wife Margrit had three children. In early 1940, the year when the Nazis took Joseph away to prison, Ruth the eldest was nearly thirteen, Edek was eleven, and the fair-haired Bronia three.

Warsaw under the Nazis was a place of terror, and without their father to protect them the Balickis had a grim time of it. But worse was in store for them. They were to endure hardships and conditions which made them think and plan and act more like adults than children.

⋆ ⋆ ⋆

It took Joseph four and a half weeks to walk to Warsaw. He had lived in the city all his life and knew it well. But now, on his return, there was hardly a

street he recognized and not an undamaged building anywhere. The place was as bleak and silent as the craters of the moon. Instead of proud homes, he found crumbling walls; instead of streets, tracks of rubble between mountains of bricks. Windows were charred and glassless. Public buildings were burnt-out shells.

In this wilderness people still managed to go on living. Joseph saw them wandering, pale and hungry-eyed, and vanish down paths of their own into the ruins. They had made their homes in cellars or had dug caves in the rubble. A few had even tried to make them look gay. A bomb gash in a cellar wall was draped with bright curtains. In another hole there was a window-box full of purple crocuses. Here and there a tree that had escaped blast damage sprouted with spring leaves.

But the only really lively place was the railway. The Nazis had to keep this clear, whatever the cost. Never had Joseph seen railway lines gleam as these did—eight lines of polished steel along which, day and night, the busy trains poured. Eastwards, with carriages of troops and trucks of ammunition, they carried war to Russia. Westwards they brought back the wounded to Germany, and sometimes rich plunder from the Ukraine.

Joseph spent three days finding the street where he used to live. The school and schoolhouse—his home—had disappeared.

There was a house opposite with a sign marked POLISH WELFARE. He made some enquiries there, but the people were new and could not help him. At another house he had better luck. He knew the woman who lived there—a Mrs Krause, who had had a child at his school some years ago. In a small back room he questioned her eagerly about his family.

'The Nazis destroyed your school,' she said.

'What happened to my wife?'

'They came for her in January last year, during the night. It was just after Dr Frank called for a million foreign workers to go to Germany. She's in Germany, probably working on the land. I'm a member of the Polish Council for Protection and we tried to trace her, but without success.'

'And the children—did they go with her?' asked Joseph.

Mrs Krause turned away. 'I don't know anything about them,' she said.

Joseph felt that she was hiding unpleasant news. He begged her to speak.

'I know nothing,' she said.

'That's not true,' he said. 'As a member of the Council, you must have found out something.'

At last, with a weary sigh, she told him all she knew. 'On the night your wife was taken away, someone fired at the van from the attic of your house. A tyre was punctured and one of the Nazi soldiers was hit in the arm. But they got away with the van all the same. An hour later they sent a truckload of soldiers with explosives. They blew the whole place up. The children have not been seen since.'

Joseph was too dazed to grasp all this at once, and Mrs Krause had to repeat it. She told him of the efforts made to trace them, but it was obvious that she believed them to be dead.

Without a word Joseph got up and went out into the street.

For the rest of the day he wandered among the ruins, too dazed to think. He spent the night in the burnt-out shell of a bus station. In spite of the rain which fell through the roof, he slept.

He spent the next few days searching among the ruins for his children, with a kind of hopeless despair. At night he returned to the home of the Krauses, who fed him and gave him a bed.

One night Mrs Krause said to him, 'It's no use your going on like this. Your children are not alive. The house was locked before the soldiers left, and they must have died in the explosion. If you want to go on searching, search for your wife.'

'Germany's a large place,' said Joseph. 'What hope should I have of finding her?'

'She might escape, as you did,' said Mrs Krause. 'You must have known that something like this might happen. Did you never make any plans? Did you never fix a meeting place?'

Joseph thought for a moment. 'Yes, as a matter of fact we did. We arranged that, if we were separated, we would try to make for Switzerland. My wife is Swiss, and her parents live there still.'

Mrs Krause took his hands in hers and smiled. 'There's your answer, then. Go to Switzerland, and with God's help you will find her there.'

'But the children—they may still be here,' said Joseph.

He spent several more days looking for them.

One afternoon, while he was poking among the rubble of his old home, he found a tiny silver sword. About five inches long, it had a brass hilt engraved with a dragon breathing fire. It was a paper knife that he had once given to his wife for a birthday present.

While he was cleaning the blade on his jersey, he

noticed that he was not alone. A small ragged boy sat watching him keenly. He had fair wispy hair and unnaturally bright eyes. Under one arm he had a wooden box, under the other a bony grey kitten.

For a moment Joseph thought it was his son, Edek. Then he realized that he was too small for Edek.

He walked over and stroked the kitten.

'What's his name?' he asked.

'He hasn't got a name. He's just mine,' said the boy.

'What's *your* name?' said Joseph.

The boy pouted and hugged the wooden box under his arm. His eyes were shrewdly summing Joseph up. After a while, 'Give me that sword,' he said.

'But it's mine,' said Joseph.

'You found it on my pitch. This is my place.'

Joseph explained about his house and how this rubble was all that was left of it.

'I'll give you food for it,' said the boy, and he offered Joseph a cheese sandwich.

'I have plenty,' said Joseph. He put his hand into his pocket, but it was empty. He looked again at the boy's sandwich and saw it was one that Mrs Krause had given him that morning, only rather grubby now.

'You little pickpocket!' he laughed. But before he could grab it back, the boy had swallowed most of it himself and given the rest to the cat, which was now purring contentedly.

After a while Joseph said, 'I'm looking for my family. Ruth is the eldest—she'd be fifteen now, and tall and fair. Then Edek, he'd be thirteen. Bronia is the youngest—she'd be five.' He described them briefly, told him what he knew of their fate and asked if the boy had seen them.

The boy shrugged his shoulders. 'Warsaw is full of

lost children,' he said. 'They're dirty and starving and they all look alike.'

His words made him sound indifferent. But Joseph noticed that the boy had listened carefully and seemed to be storing up everything in the back of his mind.

'I'll give you this sword on one condition,' said Joseph. 'I'm not sure that my children *are* dead. If ever you see Ruth or Edek or Bronia, you must tell them about our meeting. Tell them I'm going to Switzerland to find their mother. To their grandparents' home. Tell them to follow as soon as they can.'

The boy grabbed the sword before Joseph had time to change his mind. He popped it into the little wooden box, picked up the cat and ran off.

'I'll tell you more about them tomorrow,' Joseph called after him. 'Meet you here in the morning—and don't let me down.'

The boy vanished.

Joseph did not expect the boy to keep his appointment with him in the morning. But he was there, sitting on the rubble with his cat and his wooden box, waiting for him.

'It's no use your trying to pick my pockets this morning,' said Joseph, sitting down beside him.

'You've pinned the flaps,' said the boy. 'But that doesn't make any difference.'

Joseph moved away a couple of paces. 'Keep your hands off,' he said. 'Now, listen. I'm starting off for Switzerland tonight. I don't want to walk all the way, so I'm going to jump a train. Where's the best place?'

'You will be caught and shot,' said the boy. 'Or you will freeze to death in the trucks. The nights are bitter. Your hair will be white with frost, your fingers will

turn to icicles. And when the Nazis find you, you will be stiff as the boards at the bottom of the truck. That is what happens to those who jump trains.'

'You seem to know a lot about it,' said Joseph.

'I have seen it,' said the boy.

'Can't be helped. I must risk it,' said Joseph. 'Better than going back to the place I've come from.'

'I'll take you to the bend where the trains slow down,' said the boy. He jumped up and began running.

Joseph had a job to keep up with him. But the boy could run and talk and point out the landmarks and stuff food into his mouth and the cat's, all at the same time.

Joseph tried to find out something about this extraordinary boy. What was his name? Where did he live? Were his parents still alive? But the boy would tell him nothing.

They came to the railway and followed the track past the station to a large bend. Here, beside a train shed, they sat down to watch.

'All the trains slow down here,' said the boy. 'You will find no better place to jump on.'

They saw several trains pass westwards. One of them was a goods train, and it went more slowly than the rest. Would there be a goods train passing that way tonight? Joseph thought he could jump it without danger.

'Let's have something to eat,' said Joseph, and he unpinned the flaps of his pockets. But his hands went straight through and came out into the daylight. He looked at the boy watching the trains, still chewing. He looked at the cat, curled and purring in the boy's lap. He knew where his sandwiches were now.

'You little devil!' he cried. 'Just wait till I catch you.'

But the boy had vanished.

He didn't see him again till after dark, after he had said goodbye to the Krauses and left their house for the last time. The boy was waiting for him at the bottom of the street.

'Ssh!' said the boy. 'We must go by the back ways—it's curfew time. If the Nazi patrols see us, they'll shoot.'

'What's all that you're carrying?' said Joseph.

He looked closer and saw that the boy's ragged shirt was stuffed with long loaves, like monster cigars.

'Mother in heaven! Where did you get all that lot from?'

'I borrowed them,' said the boy. 'I know the canteen at the Nazi barracks. There's plenty in the bakehouse there. Take them—you'll be hungry.'

'Ought to see me through to America, that lot,' said Joseph, as he took them. 'What about yourself? You've some appetite, if I remember rightly.'

'I borrow for everybody,' said the boy. 'They always send me. I'm so small I can wriggle under the barbed wire. I run so fast the soldiers can never catch me, and if—' He broke off suddenly. 'Lie down. Patrol coming.'

They dropped behind a wall and lay flat till the patrol had passed. Then they hurried by the back ways to the railway. They almost ran into another patrol, and there were shots in the darkness. But the boy knew the ruins better than the patrol, and they got away.

They came to the bend where Joseph intended to jump, and they hid beside an empty warehouse. It was drizzling. The warehouse was littered with broken glass and charred timber. It was open to the sky except at one corner, where a strip of iron roof curled over. Under this they sheltered from the wet. A train clattered by, with a churning of pistons and a great hiss

of steam. The long carriages clanked into the darkness, and the red light on the guard's van faided.

Too fast for me, thought Joseph. I must wait for a goods train.

As they sat there waiting, Joseph said, 'I have much to thank you for, and I don't even know your name.'

The boy said nothing, but went on stroking the cat.

The drizzle turned to heavy rain. The drops danced on the roof, which creaked at every gust of wind.

'Have you no parents?' said Joseph.

'I have my grey cat and this box,' he said.

'You won't come with me?' said Joseph.

The boy ignored the question. He was undoing the wooden box, and he took out the little silver sword. 'This is the best of my treasures,' he said. 'It will bring me luck. And it will bring you luck, because you gave it to me. I don't tell anybody my name—it is not safe. But because you gave me the sword and I didn't borrow it, I will tell you.' He whispered. 'It is Jan.'

'There are many Jan's in Poland, what's your surname?'

'That's all. Just Jan.'

Joseph did not question him further. 'Stay here in the dry,' he said, when it was time to go. But Jan insisted on going with him.

They crouched down beside the main track.

A train came along—was it a goods train? By the light of a signal lamp they saw red crosses painted on the carriages, streaming with rain. A hospital train. The blinds were down. Except for an occasional blur where one had worn thin, no light peeped through.

At last, when Joseph had almost given up hope, a goods train came. The first few trucks rumbled slowly past.

'Goodbye, Jan. Remember your promise. Whatever happens, I shall not forget you. God bless you.'

Joseph chose an empty truck and ran alongside at the same speed as the train. Darkness swallowed him. Jan did not see him jump.

One by one the heavy, dismal, sodden trucks clanked by. Last of all, the small red light, so dim that it hardly showed. Then the shrill note of a whistle, as the train gathered speed beyond the bend.

It was raining heavily now.

Jan was soon soaked to the skin. He hurried away through the dark streets. He had tucked the grey cat inside his jacket. It was almost as wet as he was and hardly warm at all. Under his arm he hugged the wooden box. And he thought of the silver sword inside.

What had happened to Joseph's family that night over a year ago when the Nazi storm troopers called at the schoolhouse? Was what Mrs Krause said true? Had they taken his wife away? Had they returned and blown up the house with the children in it?

This is what happened.

That night there was an inch of snow on the roofs of Warsaw. Ruth and Bronia were asleep in the bedroom next to their mother's. Edek's room was on the top floor, below the attic. He was asleep when the Nazi soldiers broke into the house, but he woke up when he heard a noise outside his door. He jumped out of bed and turned the handle. The door was locked. He shouted and banged on it with his fists, but it was no use. Then he lay down with his ear to the floor and listened. In his mother's room the men were rapping out orders, but he could not catch a word that was said.

In the ceiling was a small trapdoor that led into the

attic. A ladder lay between his bed and the wall. Quietly he removed it, hooked it under the trap, and climbed up.

Hidden between the water tank and the felt jacket round it was his rifle. He was a member of the Boys' Rifle Brigade and had used it in the siege of Warsaw. It was loaded. He took it out and quickly climbed down to his room.

The noise in the room below had stopped. Looking out of the window into the street, he saw a Nazi van waiting outside the front door. Two storm troopers were taking his mother down the steps, and she was struggling.

Quietly Edek lifted the window sash till it was half open. He dared not shoot in case he hit his mother. He had to wait till she was in the van and the doors were being closed.

His first shot hit a soldier in the arm. Yelling, he jumped in beside the driver. With the next two shots Edek aimed at the tyres. One punctured the rear wheel, but the van got away, skidding and roaring up the street. His other shots went wide.

With the butt of his rifle he broke down the door and ran down to his sisters. They were locked in, too. He burst open the door.

Bronia was sitting up in bed and Ruth was trying to calm her. She was almost as distraught herself. Only the effort to comfort Bronia kept her from losing control.

'I hit one of the swine,' said Edek.

'That was very silly of you,' said Ruth. 'They'll come back for us now.'

'I couldn't let them take Mother away like that,' said Edek. 'Oh, be quiet, Bronia! Howling won't help.'

'We must get away from here before they come back,' said Ruth.

With some difficulty she dressed Bronia, while Edek went into the hall to fetch overcoats and boots and fur caps.

There was no time for Ruth to dress properly. She put on a coat over her nightdress and wound a woollen scarf round Bronia.

'We can't get out the front way,' said Edek. 'There's another van coming. I heard the whistle.'

'What about the back?' said Ruth.

'The wall's too high. We'd never get Bronia over. Besides, there are Nazis billeted in that street. There's only one way—over the roof.'

'We'll never manage that,' said Ruth.

'It's the only way,' said Edek. 'I'll carry Bronia. Be quick—I can bear them coming.'

He picked up the sobbing Bronia and led the way upstairs. He was wearing his father's thick overcoat over his pyjamas, a pair of stout boots on his bare feet, and his rifle slung on his back.

When they were all up in the attic, he smashed the skylight.

'Now listen, Bronia,' said Edek. 'If you make a sound, we shall never see Mother again. We shall all be killed.'

'Of course we shall see her again,' Ruth added. 'But only if you do as Edek says.'

He climbed through the skylight on to the slippery roof. Ruth handed Bronia up to him, then followed herself. The bitterly cold air made her gasp.

'I can't carry you yet, Bronia,' said Edek. 'You must walk behind me and hold on to the rifle. It doesn't matter if you slip, if you hold on to the rifle. And don't look down.'

The first few steps—as far as the V between the chimney and the roof ridge—were ghastly. Edek made

a dash for it, grabbed the telephone bracket and hauled himself up, with Bronia clinging on behind. She was speechless with terror. He reached back and hauled Ruth up after him.

After a few moments' rest, they slid down a few feet on to a flat part that jutted out, a sort of parapet.

The roof ridge lay between them and the street, so they could not see what was happening down there. But they could hear shouting, the whine of cars, the screech of brakes.

Luckily for them, all the houses on this side of the school were joined together in one long terrace, otherwise they could not have got away. Even so, it was a miracle that none of their slips and tumbles ended in disaster.

They must have gone fully a hundred yards when the first explosion shook the air. A sheet of fire leapt up from their home into the frosty night sky. They fell flat in the snow and lay there. The roof shook, the whole city seemed to tremble. Another explosion. Smoke and flames poured from the windows. Sparks showered into the darkness.

'Come along,' said Edek. 'We shan't let them have us now.'

With growing confidence they hurried along the rooftops. At last, by descending a twisted fire escape, they reached street level. On and on they hurried, not knowing or caring where they went so long as they left those roaring flames behind them.

They did not stop till the fire was far away and the pale winter dawn was breaking.

They took shelter in the cellar of a bombed house. Exhausted, huddled together for warmth, they slept till long after midday, when cold and hunger woke them.

They made their new home in a cellar at the other end of the city. They had tunnelled their way into it. From the street it looked like a rabbit's burrow in a mound of rubble, with part of a wall rising behind. On the far side there was a hole in the lower part of the wall, and this let in light and air as well as rain.

When they asked the Polish Council of Protection about their mother, they were told she had been taken off to Germany to work on the land. Nobody could say which part of Germany. Though they went many times to ask, they never found out any more. 'The war will end soon,' they were told. 'Be patient, and your mother will come back.'

But the war dragged on, and their patience was to be sorely tried.

They quickly made their new home as comfortable as they could. Edek, who could climb like a monkey, scaled three storeys of a bombed building to fetch a mattress and some curtains. The mattress he gave to Ruth and Bronia. The curtains made good sheets. On wet days they could be used over the hole in the wall to keep the rain out. With floorboards he made two beds, chairs, and a table. With bricks from the rubble he built a wall to divide the cellar into two rooms, one to live in and one to sleep in. He stole blankets from a Nazi supply dump, one for each of them.

Here they lived for the rest of that winter and the following spring.

Food was not easy to find. Ruth and Bronia had green Polish ration cards and were allowed to draw the small rations that the Nazis allowed. But, except when Edek found casual work, they had no money to buy food. Edek had no ration card. He had not dared to

apply for one, as that would have meant disclosing his age. Everyone over twelve had to register, and he would almost certainly have been carried off to Germany as a slave worker. Whenever possible they ate at the soup kitchens which Polish Welfare had set up. Sometimes they begged at a nearby convent. Sometimes they stole from the Nazis or scrounged from their garbage bins. They saw nothing wrong in stealing from their enemies, but they were careful never to steal from their own people.

In the early summer they left the city and went to live in the woods outside. It was cold at night out in the open. They slept huddled together in their blankets under an oak tree which Edek had chosen for the shelter of its branches. There was not much rain that summer, though they had one or two drenchings in May. After that Edek cut down some branches, lashed them together and made a lean-to. This was thick enough to keep out all but the heaviest rain.

Life was much healthier here than in the city. The sun browned their limbs. There were plenty of other families to play with, some of them Jews who had escaped from the Warsaw ghetto. They could run about freely and hold their classes under the trees, without having to keep a look-out for police patrols. Ruth had started a school. Sometimes she had as many as twenty-five in her school. She would have taken more, but they had no paper, very few slates, and no books at all. Occasionally they received a smuggled copy of a secret journal specially published for children by the Polish Underground press. It was called *Biedronka*, 'The Ladybird', and was full of the kind of stories and pictures and jokes that children enjoy. The grubby finger marks showed that other families had seen it before them. When Ruth's children

had finished with it, there was nothing left but a few tattered strips.

Because of the kindness of the peasants, food was more plentiful. Though they were forbidden to store food or to sell it to anyone but the Nazis, they gave the children whatever they could spare. They hid it, too, in cellars, in haystacks, in holes in the ground. With the help of the older children they smuggled it to the towns and sold it to the Poles on the black market.

Edek was one of the chief smugglers. In return for his services, he was given all the food he needed for the family. One of his dodges was to go off to town with pats of butter sewn into the lining of his coat. But he could only do this on cool days or at night. On hot days the butter melted. So he preferred to work at night if he could. In time the Germans became wary and posted patrols on all the main roads into the city. After that he cut across country, using paths and rough tracks. He was well aware of the penalties if he was caught. A younger child might get away with a beating. But boys as strong as he was would be carried off to Germany, for the Nazis were getting short of labour at home.

Another of Edek's dodges was the cartload of logs which he drove into the suburbs.

Some of the logs were split, their centres scraped out and packed with butter and eggs, then glued together again. Once he drove his cartload into a police patrol, which was searching everything on the road. They emptied the logs on to the pavement. Edek didn't stay to see if the glue would stand up to that treatment. He dived into the crowd and made off. Police whistles were blowing and the chase had started, when some kind friend lifted him up and pitched him head first into a garbage cart. Here he lay hidden, under cinders and dust and rotting vegetables.

After that, Edek did all his smuggling at night.

There came a morning, towards the end of August, when he failed to return. Ruth questioned other families in the forest, but no one had seen him. After some days of searching, she traced him to a village ten miles away. Edek had called at a house there while the secret police were searching for hidden stores. They had found cheese sewn into the lining of his coat. After setting fire to the house, they had taken him away in the van, with the house owner as well.

Ruth returned to the forest with a heavy heart, dreading to break the news to Bronia.

Edek had been their life-line. Food, clothes, money—they depended on him for all these. In the city he had made a home out of a ruin. In the woods no tree gave better shelter than the oak he had chosen. And after dark, when the wind blew cold and the damp oozed out of the ground, none knew better than he how to keep the fire in untended till dawn, so that the glow from the embers should warm them all night as they slept.

Now Ruth and Bronia must fend for themselves. It was an ordeal before which the bravest spirit might quail.

Wait For Me

Wait for me, and I'll come back,
Wait and I will come.
Wait through autumn's yellow rains
And its tedium.
Steel your heart and do not grieve,
Wait through winter's haze,
Wait through wind and raging storm,
Wait through summer's blaze.
Wait when others wait no more,
When my letters stop,
Wait with hope that never wanes,
Wait and don't give up. . . .

Wait for me! Let those who don't—
Once I'm back with you—
Let them say that it was luck
That had seen us through.
You and I alone will know
That I safely came,
Spiting every kind of death,
Through that lethal flame,
Just because you learned to wait
Staunchly, stubbornly,
And like no one else on earth
Waited, love, for me.

Konstantin Simonov

Konstantin Simonov (1915–1985) worked as a war correspondent during World War II. His poem *Zhdi menya* (*Wait For Me*) was the best-known Russian poem of the war.

from *The Diary of a Young Girl*

ANNE FRANK

Anne Frank, a Jewish girl living in Amsterdam, was thirteen when she began her diary in June 1942. The city, like all the Netherlands, was under Nazi German occupation. With her family and friends she was in hiding in a secret annexe of a house. She was fifteen when she made the last entry in her diary on 1 August 1944.

On 4 August, the eight people in hiding were arrested and deported to Auschwitz concentration camp; from there she and her sister Margot were sent on to the Belsen camp. There they both died of typhus sometime in late February or early March—just one month before the camp was liberated by British troops on 12 April 1945.

Anne's father Otto Frank was the only one of the eight to survive. He published his daughter's diary as *The Diary of a Young Girl* in 1947.

'My Dearest Kitty' is an imaginary girl friend for whom Anne wrote her diary. The people she refers to are as follows:

Mr van Hoeven ('the van Hoeven business') is a Dutchman arrested for hiding two Jews in his house; he also helped Anne and the other seven Jews in the annexe.

Peter is the son of Mr van Daan and Petronella van Daan, all three hiding in the annexe and all arrested with Anne and killed in the camps.

Margot is Anne's sister, Otto and Edith their father and mother. Only Otto survived.

The remaining Jew hiding with them was Albert Dussel, who died in a concentration camp in 1944.

Also living in the house were two female secretaries, Miep Gies and Bep Voskuijl, who did what they could to help the Jews, as did Victor Kugler and Johannes Kleimann. The secretaries escaped arrest, but the two men were put in prison in Amsterdam—both survived.

Mouschi and Moortje are cats.

It was Miep who found Anne Frank's diaries, scattered all over the floor after the police had left. She put them in a drawer until the war was over, then handed them over to Anne's father.

FRIDAY, 26 MAY 1944

My dearest Kitty,

At long, long last, I can sit quietly at my table before the crack in the window frame and write you everything, everything I want to say.

I feel more miserable than I have in months. Even after the break-in I didn't feel so utterly broken, inside and out. On the one hand, there's the news about Mr van Hoeven, the Jewish question (which is discussed in detail by everyone in the house), the invasion (which is so long in coming), the awful food, the tension, the miserable atmosphere, my disappointment in Peter. On the other hand, there's Bep's engagement, the Whitsun reception, the flowers, Mr Kugler's birthday, cakes and stories about cabarets, films and concerts. That gap, that enormous gap, is always there. One day we're

laughing at the comical side of life in hiding, and the next day (and there are many such days), we're frightened, and the fear, tension, and despair can be read on our faces.

Miep and Mr Kugler bear the greatest burden for us, and for all those in hiding—Miep in everything she does and Mr Kugler through his enormous responsibility for the eight of us, which is sometimes so overwhelming that he can hardly speak from the pent-up tension and strain. Mr Kleiman and Bep also take very good care of us, but they're able to put the Annexe out of their minds, even if it's only for a few hours or a few days. They have their own worries, Mr Kleiman with his health and Bep with her engagement, which isn't looking very promising at the moment. But they also have their outings, their visits to friends, their everyday lives as ordinary people, so that the tension is sometimes relieved, if only for a short while, while ours never is, never has been, not once in the two years we've been here. How much longer will this increasingly oppressive, unbearable weight press down on us?

The drains are clogged again. We can't run the water, or if we do, only a trickle; we can't flush the toilet, so we have to use a toilet brush; and we've been putting our dirty water into a big earthenware jar. We can manage for today, but what will happen if the plumber can't mend it on his own? They can't come to do the drains until Tuesday.

Miep sent us a currant loaf with 'Happy Whitsun' written on top. It's almost as if she were mocking us, since our moods and cares are far from 'happy'.

We've all become more frightened since the van Hoeven business. Once again you hear 'shh' from all sides, and we're doing everything more quietly. The

police forced the door there; they could just as easily do that here too! What will we do if we're ever . . . no, I mustn't write that down. But the question won't let itself be pushed to the back of my mind today; on the contrary, all the fear I've ever felt is looming before me in all its horror.

I had to go downstairs alone at eight this evening to use the lavatory. There was no one down there, since they were all listening to the radio. I wanted to be brave, but it was hard. I always feel safer upstairs than in that huge, silent house; when I'm alone with those mysterious muffled sounds from upstairs and the honking of horns in the street, I have to hurry and remind myself where I am to keep from getting the shivers.

Miep has been acting much nicer towards us since her talk with Father. But I haven't told you about that yet. Miep came up one afternoon all flushed and asked Father straight out if we thought they too were infected with the current anti-Semitism. Father was stunned and quickly talked her out of the idea, but some of Miep's suspicion has lingered on. They're doing more errands for us now and showing more of an interest in our troubles, though we certainly shouldn't bother them with our woes. Oh, they're such good, noble people!

I've asked myself again and again whether it wouldn't have been better if we hadn't gone into hiding, if we were dead now and didn't have to go through this misery, especially so that the others could be spared the burden. But we all shrink from this thought. We still love life, we haven't yet forgotten the voice of nature, and we keep hoping, hoping for . . . everything.

Let something happen soon, even an air raid.

Nothing can be more crushing than this anxiety. Let the end come, however cruel; at least then we'll know whether we are to be the victors or the vanquished.

Yours, Anne M. Frank

FRIDAY, 2 JUNE 1944

Dear Kitty,

If you're going to the attic, take an umbrella with you, preferably a large one! This is to protect you from 'household showers'. There's a Dutch proverb: 'High and dry, safe and sound', but it obviously doesn't apply to wartime (guns!) and to people in hiding (litter box!). Mouschi's got into the habit of relieving herself on some newspapers or between the cracks in the floorboards, so we have good reason to fear the splatters and, even worse, the stench. The new Moortje in the warehouse has the same problem. Anyone who's ever had a cat that's not housebroken can imagine the smells, other than pepper and thyme, that permeate this house.

I also have a brand-new prescription for gunfire jitters: when the shooting gets loud, proceed to the nearest wooden staircase. Run up and down a few times, making sure to stumble at least once. What with the scratches and the noise of running and falling, you won't even be able to hear the shooting, much less worry about it. Yours truly has put this magic formula to use, with great success!

Yours, Anne M. Frank

TUESDAY, 13 JUNE 1944

Dearest Kit,

Another birthday has gone by, so I'm now fifteen. I

received quite a few gifts: Springer's five-volume art history book, a set of underwear, two belts, a handkerchief, two pots of yoghurt, a pot of jam, two honey biscuits (small), a botany book from Father and Mother, a gold bracelet from Margot, a sticker album from the van Daans, Biomalt and sweet peas from Dussel, sweets from Miep, sweets and exercise-books from Bep, and the high point: the book *Maria Theresa* and three slices of full-cream cheese from Mr Kugler. Peter gave me a lovely bouquet of peonies; the poor boy had put a lot of effort into finding a present, but nothing quite worked out.

Why is it, I often ask myself, that everyone still thinks I'm so pushy and such a know-it-all? Am I really so arrogant? Am *I* the one who's so arrogant, or are they? It sounds silly, I know, but I'm not going to cross out that last sentence, because it's not as silly as it seems. Mrs van Daan and Dussel, my two chief accusers, are known to be totally unintelligent and, not to put too fine a point on it, just plain 'stupid'! Stupid people usually can't bear it when others do something better than they do; the best examples of this are those two dunces, Mrs van Daan and Dussel. Mrs van D. thinks I'm stupid because I don't suffer so much from this ailment as she does, she thinks I'm pushy because she's even pushier, she thinks my dresses are too short because hers are even shorter, and she thinks I'm such a know-it-all because she talks twice as much as I do about topics she knows nothing about. The same goes for Dussel. But one of my favourite sayings is 'Where there's smoke there's fire', and I readily admit I'm a know-it-all.

What's so difficult about my personality is that I scold and curse myself much more than anyone else does; if Mother adds her advice, the pile of sermons

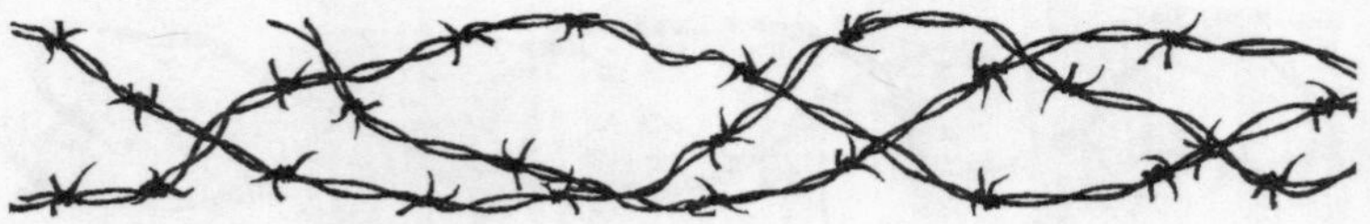

becomes so thick that I despair of ever getting through them. Then I talk back and start contradicting everyone until the old familiar Anne refrain inevitably crops up again: 'No one understands me!'

This phrase is part of me, and, as unlikely as it may seem, there's a kernel of truth in it. Sometimes I'm so deeply buried under self-reproaches that I long for a word of comfort to help me dig myself out again. If only I had someone who took my feelings seriously. Alas, I haven't yet found that person, so the search must go on.

I know you're wondering about Peter, aren't you, Kit? It's true, Peter loves me, not as a girlfriend, but as a friend. His affection grows day by day, but some mysterious force is holding us back, and I don't know what it is.

Sometimes I think my terrible longing for him was over-exaggerated. But that's not true, because if I'm unable to go to his room for a day or two, I long for him as desperately as I ever did. Pcter is kind and good, and yet I can't deny that he's disappointed me in many ways. I especially don't care for his dislike of religion, his talk of food and various things of that nature. Still, I'm firmly convinced that we'll stick to our agreement never to quarrel. Peter is peace-loving, tolerant, and extremely easy-going. He lets me say a lot of things to him that he'd never accept from his mother. He's making a determined effort to remove the blots from his copybook and keep his affairs in order. Yet why does he hide his innermost self and never allow me access? Of course, he's much more closed than I am, but I know from experience (even though I'm constantly being accused of knowing all there is to know in theory, but not in practice) that in time, even the most uncommunicative types will

long as much, or even more, for someone to confide in.

Peter and I have both spent our contemplative years in the Annexe. We often discuss the future, the past, and the present, but as I've already told you, I miss the real thing, and yet I know it exists!

Is it because I haven't been outdoors for so long that I've become so mad about nature? I remember a time when a magnificent blue sky, chirping birds, moonlight, and budding blossoms wouldn't have captivated me. Things have changed since I came here. One night during Whitsun, for instance, when it was so hot, I struggled to keep my eyes open until eleven-thirty so I could get a good look at the moon, all on my own for once. Alas, my sacrifice was in vain, since there was too much glare and I couldn't risk opening a window. Another time, several months ago, I happened to be upstairs one night when the window was open. I didn't go back down until it had to be closed again. The dark, rainy evening, the wind, the racing clouds, had me spellbound; it was the first time in a year and a half that I'd seen the night face-to-face. After that evening my longing to see it again was even greater than my fear of burglars, a dark rat-infested house or police raids. I went downstairs all by myself and looked out of the windows in the kitchen and private office. Many people think nature is beautiful, many people sleep from time to time under the starry sky, and many people in hospitals and prisons long for the day when they'll be free to enjoy what nature has to offer. But few are as isolated and cut off as we are from the joys of nature, which can be shared by rich and poor alike.

It's not just my imagination—looking at the sky, the

clouds, the moon and the stars really does make me feel calm and hopeful. It's much better medicine than valerian or bromide. Nature makes me feel humble and ready to face every blow with courage!

As luck would have it, I'm only able—except for a few rare occasions—to view nature through dusty curtains tacked over dirt-caked windows; it takes the pleasure out of looking. Nature is the one thing for which there is no substitute!

One of the many questions that have often bothered me is why women have been, and still are, thought to be so inferior to men. It's easy to say it's unfair, but that's not enough for me; I'd really like to know the reason for this great injustice!

Men presumably dominated women from the very beginning because of their greater physical strength; it's men who earn a living, beget children, and do as they please . . . Until recently, women silently went along with this, which was stupid, since the longer it's kept up, the more deeply entrenched it becomes. Fortunately, education, work and progress have opened women's eyes. In many countries they've been granted equal rights; many people, mainly women, but also men, now realize how wrong it was to tolerate this state of affairs for so long. Modern women want the right to be completely independent!

But that's not all. Women should be respected as well! Generally speaking, men are held in great esteem in all parts of the world, so why shouldn't women have their share? Soldiers and war heroes are honoured and commemorated, explorers are granted immortal fame, martyrs are revered, but how many people look upon women too as soldiers?

In the book *Men against Death* I was greatly struck by the fact that in childbirth alone, women commonly suffer more pain, illness, and misery than any war hero ever does. And what's her reward for enduring all that pain? She gets pushed aside when she's disfigured by birth, her children soon leave, her beauty is gone. Women, who struggle and suffer pain to ensure the continuation of the human race, make much tougher and more courageous soldiers than all those big-mouthed freedom-fighting heroes put together!

I don't mean to imply that women should stop having children; on the contrary, nature intended them to, and that's the way it should be. What I condemn are our system of values and the men who don't acknowledge how great, difficult, but ultimately beautiful women's share in society is.

I agree completely with Paul de Kruif, the author of this book, when he says that men must learn that birth is no longer thought of as inevitable and unavoidable in those parts of the world we consider civilized. It's easy for men to talk—they don't and never will have to bear the woes that women do!

I believe that in the course of the next century the notion that it's a woman's duty to have children will change and make way for the respect and admiration of all women, who bear their burdens without complaint or a lot of pompous words!

Yours, Anne M. Frank

TUESDAY, 1 AUGUST 1944

Dearest Kitty,

'A bundle of contradictions' was the end of my previous letter and is the beginning of this one. Can

you please tell me exactly what 'a bundle of contradictions' is? What does 'contradiction' mean? Like so many words, it can be interpreted in two ways: a contradiction imposed from without and one imposed from within. The former means not accepting other people's opinions, always knowing best, having the last word; in short, all those unpleasant traits for which I'm known. The latter, for which I'm not known, is my own secret.

As I've told you many times, I'm split in two. One side contains my exuberant cheerfulness, my flippancy, my joy in life and, above all, my ability to appreciate the lighter side of things. By that I mean not finding anything wrong with flirtations, a kiss, an embrace, a saucy joke. This side of me is usually lying in wait to ambush the other one, which is much purer, deeper and finer. No one knows Anne's better side, and that's why most people can't stand me. Oh, I can be an amusing clown for an afternoon, but after that everyone's had enough of me to last a month. Actually, I'm what a romantic film is to a profound thinker—a mere diversion, a comic interlude, something that is soon forgotten: not bad, but not particularly good either. I hate having to tell you this, but why shouldn't I admit it when I know it's true? My lighter, more superficial side will always steal a march on the deeper side and therefore always win. You can't imagine how often I've tried to push away this Anne, which is only half of what is known as Anne—to beat her down, hide her. But it doesn't work, and I know why.

I'm afraid that people who know me as I usually am will discover I have another side, a better and finer side. I'm afraid they'll mock me, think I'm ridiculous and sentimental and not take me seriously. I'm used to not being taken seriously, but only the 'lighthearted'

Anne is used to it and can put up with it; the 'deeper' Anne is too weak. If I force the good Anne into the spotlight for even fifteen minutes, she shuts up like a clam the moment she's called upon to speak, and lets Anne number one do the talking. Before I realize it, she's disappeared.

So the nice Anne is never seen in company. She's never made a single appearance, though she almost always takes the stage when I'm alone. I know exactly how I'd like to be, how I am . . . on the inside. But unfortunately I'm only like that with myself. And perhaps that's why—no, I'm sure that's the reason why—I think of myself as happy on the inside and other people think I'm happy on the outside. I'm guided by the pure Anne within, but on the outside I'm nothing but a frolicsome little goat tugging at its tether.

As I've told you, what I say is not what I feel, which is why I have a reputation for being a boy-chaser, a flirt, a smart aleck and a reader of romances. The happy-go-lucky Anne laughs, gives a flippant reply, shrugs her shoulders and pretends she couldn't care less. The quiet Anne reacts in just the opposite way. If I'm being completely honest, I'll have to admit that it does matter to me, that I'm trying very hard to change myself, but that I'm always up against a more powerful enemy.

A voice within me is sobbing, 'You see, that's what's become of you. You're surrounded by negative opinions, dismayed looks and mocking faces, people who dislike you, and all because you don't listen to the advice of your own better half.' Believe me, I'd like to listen, but it doesn't work, because if I'm quiet and serious, everyone thinks I'm putting on a new act and I have to save myself with a joke, and then I'm not even

talking about my own family, who assume I must be ill, stuff me with aspirins and sedatives, feel my neck and forehead to see if I have a temperature, ask about my bowel movements and berate me for being in a bad mood, until I just can't keep it up any more, because when everybody starts hovering over me, I get cross, then sad, and finally end up turning my heart inside out, the bad part on the outside and the good part on the inside, and keep trying to find a way to become what I'd like to be and what I could be if . . . if only there were no other people in the world.

Yours, Anne M. Frank

ANNE'S DIARY ENDS HERE

8th May 1945

Hasty is the flight of birds. Woe, all that was ever
  ready to soar
Has the weight of stones
That endure under the earth, cemented with the
  bodies and years of love.

People have buried their wickedly pampered war.
Poppies bloom out of beer.
Paper-chains lace up the bodies of feverish houses.

The wet flags drip into sultry, festive air.
Behind the roll of drums
A skater zigzags over a frozen lake of blood.

Franz Baermann Steiner

Franz Baermann Steiner (1909–1952) was a German Jewish poet whose parents both died in concentration camps in 1942.

from *A Time of Fire*

ROBERT WESTALL

The English writer Robert Westall wrote several well-loved books (*The Machine Gunners*, *Echoes of War*) based loosely on his boyhood memories of World War II, when he was growing up in the north-east of England. In this story, a German plane bombs the town before being shot down. The pilot, however, escapes by parachute and bursts into the house where Sonny is living with his grandad . . .

He whipped inside and grabbed Granda's old night-glasses, from where they hung on the back of the door. Focused frantically; the dark river, the piers, the lighthouses leaping around before his eyes like fleas. He just caught the black figure of the parachutist as it plunged into the smooth waters of the harbour. The canopy of the parachute ghosted down gently on top, and lay flat on the water. There was no sign of life underneath it; only the widening rings of ripples on the smooth oily water.

Perhaps he was dead before he hit the water, thought

Sonny. Or wounded. Perhaps he's drowning now. He felt nothing but a fascinated coldness; like when he'd watched a spider, in Granda's shed, trap and kill a big bluebottle.

There was suddenly a hump under the parachute, as the man surfaced and struggled to free himself. Then he broke out in a flurry of foam and frantic arms and legs. Sonny could see quite clearly, through the glasses, the tight German flying-helmet that made his head look like a seal's. The RAF had quite different sorts of helmets, more domed and bumpy . . .

So, he was alive. But the sailors on the boom-defence across the harbour mouth would have seen him. The boom-defence launch would be on its way to pick him up, any minute . . .

But nothing stirred from the boom. No sound of any chugging diesel engine. The sailors must all be watching the raid, as it roared upriver in a blizzard of gigantic fireworks, arcs of dull red tracer climbing ever so slowly up into the sky, the smaller golden balls from the pompoms.

The Jerry was free of his parachute now. He was looking around, working out which land was nearest.

And on the nearest land to him was the Old Coastguard Station. Quite calmly, Sonny knew he would come. If he didn't drown on the way. God was setting his mousetrap . . . It all seemed inevitable now, from the beginning. A trap slowly working out.

Granda's shotgun stood in the corner handy, by the fireplace. But where were the shells? Granda always kept them hidden away. He said he didn't want any nasty accidents . . .

Hopelessly, Sonny pulled out all the kitchen drawers, but there were only knives and forks and spoons, corkscrews and funny old bits of metal from

the far past with no names. Then he pulled out the drawers in the sideboard. But that was just draughts sets and dominoes and table-mats. The photographs of Mam, and Dad in his uniform with his corporal's stripes, smiled at him from the sideboard top.

No good. But the Jerry mustn't have the shotgun. Sonny ran outside with it, and hid it behind the rainwater-butt. Then he remembered the bottles of petrol, with the rags in the top; the Molotov cocktails . . .

He did not quite see how they could be used. But he quickly took two, and hid them under the sink, behind Nana's waste-bucket.

The night had gone very quiet now. Just flickers and thuds in the distance, and the usual pink glow growing over the docks upriver. He took the night-glasses to the garden wall, and searched the waters of the harbour, and finally found a black seal-like blob, moving ahead of a dark arrowhead of ripples. He must keep the Jerry in sight, all the way. He must not lose sight of him again. It was tense and exciting, like when he was out hunting rats in the shipyard with Dad.

So he watched the Jerry wading ashore across the flat rocks, where Dad had shot the seagulls so long ago. First the shoulders, and then the bulky flying suit that made him look like a bear, a bear coming dripping out of the water. The cliff was about fifty feet high at this point, soft brown crumbling soil, loosened by the rain, and made slippery by the Jerry's own drippings. He heard the man swear in German, as his feet slipped away from under him, and he slid full-length back to the rocks. A giggle grew in his throat, but he pressed his lips tight closed, and no sound came out.

The German was a long time climbing the cliff; he made very heavy weather of it, grunting and gasping

and swearing. But at last he levered himself on to the grass of the cliff-edge, and Sonny knew it was time to slip noiselessly back into the house.

He did consider running to warn the sentries. But they would just come and take the man away, and that would be the end of it. And somehow, he knew, that was not the end that was meant for this one . . .

He ran upstairs, and peeped out of the window of Nana's darkened bedroom, where the blackout was not drawn. Watched the Jerry's shambling approach. The Jerry reached the gate and seemed to hesitate. He looked hard towards the pier-approach. But then he seemed to see the wire and the sentries, and the next moment he was moving silently up the garden path.

Sonny ran downstairs and into the kitchen, and sat in a chair by the now-blazing fire. He did not want to give Jerry a fright. Jerry might have a pistol. They said they carried pistols, just like British aircrew. Sonny had no wish to get shot by accident, before he had done what he had to do.

He heard the back door start to creak cautiously open. Again, he had the impulse to giggle. Jerry thought he was being so clever . . . Sonny picked up his copy of the *Wizard* and pretended to be deep in it.

The kitchen door swung open. Sonny looked up.

The Jerry was huge; he filled the doorway, muddy and black and shining and dripping on to Nana's lino. He trailed tentacles from his body, with little tiny bits of shiny metal on the ends. His bright yellow life-jacket was inflated, making him look even bigger. And he didn't look human, with that tight leather flying-helmet crushing his skull in, so that only his green eyes showed, and his long pale nose, and his mouth, gaping like a fish's, showing green tombstone teeth.

And in his left hand, the pistol Sonny had been

expecting. A Luger automatic. He recognized it from the picture in *War Weekly*. And the cocking-handle was pulled right back, and the round black hole in the end of the barrel pointed straight at the *Wizard*, held in front of Sonny's midriff.

'Odders?' he shouted. 'Udders . . . odders . . . others?' He stared round him wildly, eyes wide, ears cocked.

Sonny knew what he meant. Was there anybody else in the house?

'*Nein*,' he said. That was what they said in the war comics. He felt a little glow of pride. Till the German grabbed him up roughly, and thrust him out into the hall in front of him, using him as a human shield. Shouting '*'Raus, 'raus!*' and pushing him cruelly, when he moved too slowly.

They went through the dark empty bedrooms. Then the rooms in the watch-tower. His own room, with the Jerry still dripping on a comic he'd left on the floor. Then the very top, the balcony. Outside, the gun-flashes seemed to be moving south; the rest of the Jerry bombers were going home another way. It must make Jerry feel a bit lonely. He alone was left.

Like the last Norseman must have felt, when they hunted him down, and nailed his skin to the church door, so long ago.

Now Sonny was being bundled downstairs again. He was pushed so roughly that he fell and slid down four stairs. The huge cruel hand dragged him upright, belted him one across the ear. '*'Raus, 'raus!*'

The Jerry saw the cellar door, slightly ajar. He pushed Sonny towards it.

'Don't *push*!' shouted Sonny. 'The stairs are steep.'

He was still shoved down them. He landed on all fours at the bottom, and hurt his knees.

The Jerry glanced round, at the sacks and bottles and Granda's scythe hanging on the whitewashed wall. He was still glancing round when a small and furious bundle, barking like a fiend, hurled itself at his ankle.

The Jerry swore, struck down with the gun, making Blitz yelp. Two more savage blows, two more yelps, and then the Jerry kicked his foot and Blitz flew across the room, hit the wall with a thud, and lay silent, in a pathetically small heap.

That was the point when Sonny made up his mind the Jerry must *die*. His mind had been a bit wild and fuzzy till then, but now it was quite hard and firm and cold. It was just a matter of waiting for a chance . . .

The Jerry was staring at Grimalkin; who was glaring back, hunched on the table, ears flattened. Grimalkin spat; the Jerry raised the pistol, then appeared to change his mind, and bundled Sonny back upstairs. He sat down in a rocker in the kitchen, and seemed to relax, now he knew the house was empty. He pulled off his flying-helmet. It didn't make him look any prettier. He had blond hair, not cropped, but long and greasy as if it hadn't been washed for a month. And his green eyes were too close together. Nana always said you should never trust a man whose eyes were too close together.

The Jerry pointed the gun at Sonny and shouted, 'Fut . . . fud . . . ' He pointed at his mouth, and pretended to munch his big tombstone teeth.

What could Sonny do but go to the larder? Get the half-loaf that would have to do supper and tomorrow's breakfast. The butter-dish from the top shelf, with the remains of the week's ration of butter and marge, mixed up together to last longer. He began to cut a thin slice, but the Jerry pushed him aside, cut the loaf in half, smeared all the butter and marge on it, and the

remains of a jar of jam that his green eyes had spotted. He put the gun down and began to tear the bread off in large chunks and stuff them in his mouth.

Sonny eyed the distance to the gun lying there. The Jerry saw him eyeing it, and moved it out of reach. When he had finished the loaf, he picked up the pistol again and went into the larder himself, groping his big hand along the shelves, picking up the cheese ration, and a couple of half-stale cakes, and stuffing them into his mouth in turn. He was gulping stuff so quickly you could tell it hurt him to swallow. But he still went on doing it. He swallowed three slightly shrivelled apples, then came across a full jar of jam and began eating it with a spoon, direct from the jar. Didn't they feed them before they went on a raid? Were the Jerries *really* starving, as the Ministry of Information used to say in the Phoney War?

Having emptied the larder, the Jerry returned to his rocking-chair. He seemed a bit calmer; he belched loudly, then grinned, trying to make a joke of it, wanting Sonny to laugh.

Sonny kept his face absolutely straight. Waiting his chance.

And when it came, it was so simple. Like a gift from the Gods.

'*Trinken*,' said the Jerry. '*Trink* . . . drink!'

Sonny kept his face straight, sullen, though his heart leapt. He made an empty gesture towards the teapot . . .

'*Nein, nein!*' roared the Jerry. '*Trink!*' He mimed the gesture of taking a cork out of a bottle; lifting the invisible bottle to his lips.

Sonny raised his eyebrows and pointed down towards the cellar. The Jerry nodded; he had seen the bottles of Nana's elderberry on the shelf down there. He lumbered

to his feet and came as far as the cellar door and watched Sonny descend.

Sonny went to Blitz first. The little dog still lay where he had fallen. In the light from the paraffin lamp, Sonny could not be sure if he was still breathing or not. He felt him; he felt warmish and floppy, but Sonny know that didn't mean anything. It took time for things to go cold and stiff, Granda said.

With tears of rage in his eyes, Sonny turned to the bottles on the shelf. There was this year's stuff, still fermenting, harmless. There was 1939, 1938, the last happy years of peace.

And there was 1937; the lethal stuff that a year ago had done such harm to the curate. It would be even stronger now. He lifted down three bottles of the 1937, and cradled them so gently in his arms as he climbed the stairs.

'*Gut*,' grunted the German. '*Gut*. Goo-od.' He made a corkscrew gesture with his free hand.

Silent and correct as a butler in a movie, Sonny fetched him the corkscrew.

The Jerry had trouble with the corkscrew; his hands were shaking. Suddenly, in a rage, he smashed the neck of the bottle against the brick surround of the range; the neck broke off, and tinkled among the ashes. Then the Jerry threw back his head, and opened his tombstone mouth, and poured half the bottle down his throat. Sonny eased himself contentedly into a chair; now it was only a matter of waiting. He thought about the petrol-bombs, the Molotov cocktails under the sink, and his stomach crawled with excitement.

The Jerry stared at the half-empty bottle. He was baffled. Elderberry tasted so fresh and harmless; the look on the Jerry's face was the same one Granda had when he said, 'Gnat's pee!'

Still, the Jerry must have been quite thirsty. He finished the bottle in three more gulps.

Helpfully, Sonny reached for the corkscrew and began to open a second bottle.

The Jerry smiled. '*Ja. Wein. Gut.*' He took the second bottle from Sonny's offering hand. He stretched out his wet legs to the blaze, and let the gun droop over the arm of the rocker. Then he had a long think, mouthing words to himself, and finally said, slowly but quite clearly, '*Englander* . . . are not our natural enemy!' He seemed very pleased with this, took another swig and announced, '*Englander* . . . little bruder . . . brothers.' He had a lot of bother with the word 'brother'. Then he put down the bottle for a minute, and reached across and patted Sonny on the knee. Then he picked up the bottle again, and offered it to Sonny, indicating that he drink too.

'Drink, little brother.'

Sonny made a mess of it. He didn't want to drink, and yet he knew he had to. Or the Jerry might suspect an attempt to poison him. So Sonny drank, and it went down the wrong way, and he sprayed it all over the place, and went into an agonizing fit of coughing.

The Jerry threw up his head and laughed as if he thought this was hilarious. He got up and banged Sonny on the back painfully. Sonny's back crept in disgust, at the touch of that hand.

'*Wein* . . . not for . . . little brother!' Oh, he thought it *such* a joke. Then he sat down again, and said, solemn as an owl, '*Englander*, little brother . . . but Europe corrupt . . . we must make a New Order. Then . . . all happy!'

Sonny just waited. The elderberry was starting to have its deadly effect. The Jerry was slumping lower in his chair. His strange speech was starting to slur, as if

his tongue and lips were getting too much to manage. And the hand that held the gun was playing with it, feverishly. Sonny grew afraid it might go off.

And then the Jerry wasn't grinning any more. He looked at Sonny like a blinking owl and said, 'Drink toast to Rudi . . . *mein Kamerad*.' Then he said, '*Rudi ist tot* . . . dead.' He blinked again, and Sonny realized suddenly he was blinking back tears. '*Und Heini ist tot. Und Maxi und Karl. Alle . . . tot*.' The tears began to stream silently down his face. '*Meine Kameraden*.' He drank heavily from the second bottle. Then he began to sing, in a maudlin dreadful voice, that cracked and broke on every phrase. Something about '*Ich hatt einen Kameraden*'. And Sonny knew he was singing about the crew of his plane.

And his heart might have softened. Until he thought of Mam and Dad and Blitz, and the God who is not mocked.

Then he just went on waiting.

Finally, the Jerry stopped. An alarmed look grew on his face. He tried to get up, and failed, the rocker swinging and slewing under him, so he fell heavily back into it. He tried again, pressing down with both hands on the chair-arms. And since he had a bottle in one hand, and the gun in the other, he didn't make it again. The hand that held the bottle opened and the bottle fell on to Nana's clippie rug with a dull clunk, and rolled towards Sonny, spilling out a trail of elderberry that stained as dark as blood.

Slowly, on the third attempt, the Jerry managed to lever himself to his feet. He stared at Sonny, his face with its gaping tombstone mouth unreadable. Sonny wondered whether he was going to be shot. Whether, in an instant, there would be a bang and an agony, then darkness and he would wake up with Mam and Dad . . .

But perhaps the Jerry remembered sending for the wine himself; sending his little slave labourer.

Instead, the Jerry made a wavering track for the door, crashing into the furniture in his way, hurting himself badly, and gasping with the pain. He reminded Sonny of something . . .

The daddy-long-legs, in the oil lamp. Like it, he had come flying in; like it, he was dashing himself to pieces. Sonny almost laughed out loud. Except that pistol was wavering all over the room . . .

Then it went off. The noise was deafening. A panel of the kitchen door suddenly ceased to exist, and splinters flew everywhere, and there was that Guy Fawkes smell, and the resinous piney smell of splintered wood.

Then the gun went off again, and the Jerry cried out. And Sonny saw blood welling from the leg of his wet flying suit. Dark red, flowing, glistening. And then, with a wild yell, he was gone out of the back door, and the wind was blowing in.

Sonny ran to the door, slipped through the blackout curtain, his hand automatically rearranging it behind him. He peered right.

Against the pink glow that was Newcastle burning, he saw the Jerry lurching like a Saturday-night drunk among the ragged Brussels sprouts of Granda's garden.

He was heading for . . . the early potato patch. From which, so long ago, he and Granda had taken the soil for the sandbags. With the coming of winter, it had filled up with water. They called it the duck-pond now. Granda had even spoken of getting a few Khaki Campbells or Aylesburys, for the eggs . . .

With a sudden coldness inside him, Sonny suddenly knew he wasn't going to need the Molotov cocktails. God's little mousetrap was going to work without him

doing anything. He only had to watch, as he had once watched the spider catch the bluebottle. God would do the rest. God was not mocked.

The Jerry, as if fated, drew nearer and nearer the edge of the hole. Once, he veered away towards safety; but as if something drew him to his fate, he wavered back. There was a gasp, a slip, a cry in German, then a splash, a huge splash. He was in. Headfirst. His gun wouldn't do him any good now, down in the water.

There were more gasps. What sounded like a cry for help.

Sonny crept closer, to watch.

A hand came in sight, above the edge of the hole. A hand grasping at the smooth muddy squelchy sides, and getting no grip and falling back again. Again, the hand appeared, and then fell back.

It did not come a third time.

Sonny crept up, and looked over the edge.

Four feet down, the water glinted; and in the water, only a series of dark humps. As he watched, a burst of greasy muddy bubbles broke the surface, from the smallest, furthest-away bump.

Just a little more waiting, and it would be over.

It was then that Sonny thought of Granda's garden; and the Old Coastguard House. Where Mam had been happy; where Mam, he was sure, still came. Where Dad might still come, in dreams.

But if the Jerry died, *he* would be in the garden. Always. You would not be able to go in the garden without looking at that patch of soil, and remembering.

He would poison the whole garden. Then there would never be happiness again. He might come in dreams, huge, dripping, muddy, trailing wires, faceless like a seal under his flying-helmet. He would make sleep unthinkable.

More bubbles broke the surface of the muddy water. Perhaps there was still time to cleanse the garden.

Sonny didn't hesitate. He leapt down into the hole, trampling on the squidgy mass that was the dying Jerry. Jerry raised his head and groaned, a dreadful noise. Sonny knelt and reached for his head, and held it above the water. But it was heavy, so heavy. Jerry wriggled, and Sonny's hand slipped, and the head went down into the black water again, and there were more bubbles.

Then he saw what he must do. Raise Jerry's head, and get his own legs under it.

It was a struggle, but at least, groaning and panting to himself, he managed it. And sat with his back braced against the side of the hole, with the freezing water creeping up to his waist, then his chest, and his own bottom squidging lower and lower into the mud, every time he tried to ease himself, under the enormous weight.

And so he sat, as the last raid droned in overhead, and the guns lit up the sky, and the searchlights searched in vain, and the shrapnel came whispering down, and even thudded once among the very Brussels sprouts behind his head. Sat, with only a faint sound of barking from the Old Coastguard Station cellar to comfort him. At least Blitz was alive, after all. There would be no more death.

And it was there, after the all-clear had gone, that Granda found him, coming in response to his faint calls, after Sonny had heard the garden gate click.

'God love the bairn!' cried Granda. 'What's this?'

'A Jerry,' gasped Sonny.

'Can ye hang on a bit?' yelled Granda. 'Aah'll fetch the sentries.'

Granda knew what he was talking about. It took the

three of them to get the Jerry out, and they had to summon an ambulance to take him away under guard to Preston Hospital. He had come round by then. From the stretcher, his huge hand grabbed Sonny's.

'*Kamerad*,' he gasped. '*Freund!*'

Sonny's face went stony, though he could not get his hand free.

'Dornier?' he asked at last, coldly. 'Dornier?'

The pilot's muddy face was a picture of bewilderment.

'*Nein*,' he said, puzzled. '*Nein*. Heinkel! Heinkel!'

Then they took him away.

Granda looked at the hole. 'By,' he said, 'aah often went fishin' as a lad, but Aah never cowt anything as big as that. Aah'll have to get that hole filled in. *Anybody* could drown in it.'

'Yes,' said Sonny, flatly. He felt so weary he could hardly stand.

They went into the kitchen. Granda looked at the shattered kitchen door, the bottle on the hearth rug, the blood on the doormat, then he noticed the two Molotov cocktails under the sink. His grey eyebrows went up, nearly vanishing under his grey hair.

'By, Aah can tell there's a tale to tell here! An' look at that dog, hoppin' around on three legs . . . '

'Yes,' said Sonny flatly.

'But here's yer Nana comin' up the path. By God, there'll be hell to pay when she sees that door.' He picked up the bottle off the hearth rug. 'We'd better get tidied up, an' save the tale till later, eh?'

And that was where they left it.

Ladybird, Ladybird

'Ladybird, ladybird,
fly away home . . . '
leopard-winged ladybirds,
why do they roam?
the children were singing
the summer refrain,
'Ladybird, ladybird,
fly home again!'

Outside, a tired woman
lingered to say,
'You wouldn't know of
a place I could stay . . . ?'
Weary, with bundles—
life had gone west.
'Bombed out last night, dear—
I—just need a rest . . . '

(Children and ladybirds
singing of flight . . .)
'I had two kiddies, dear—
until last night . . . '
Oh, ladybird, ladybird—
So it goes on—
Your house is afire
and your children are gone.

Ruth Tomalin

from *War Horse*

MICHAEL MORPURGO

In the Village Hall close to Michael Morpurgo's farm hangs a small dusty painting of a horse. The inscription says:

JOEY
Painted by Captain James Nicholls
Autumn 1914

War Horse is Joey's story, straight from 'the horse's mouth' and Michael Morpurgo's pen.

When the end of the war did come, it came swiftly, almost unexpectedly it seemed to the men around me. There was little joy, little celebration of victory, only a sense of profound relief that at last it was finished and done with. Albert left the happy cluster of men gathered together in the yard that cold November morning and strolled over to talk to me. 'Five minutes time and it'll be finished, Joey, all over. Jerry's had about enough of it, and so have we. No one really wants to go on any more. At eleven o'clock the guns

will stop and then that will be that. Only wish that David could have been here to see it.'

Since David's death Albert had not been himself. I had not once seen him smile or joke, and he often fell into prolonged brooding silences when he was with me. There was no more singing, no more whistling. I tried all that I could to comfort him, resting my head on his shoulder and nickering gently to him, but he seemed quite inconsolable. Even the news that the war was finally ending brought no light back to his eyes. The bell in the clock tower over the gateway rang out eleven times, and the men shook each other solemnly by the hand or clapped each other on the back before returning to the stables.

The fruits of victory were to prove bitter indeed for me, but to begin with the end of the war changed little. The Veterinary Hospital operated as it always had done, and the flow of sick and injured horses seemed rather to increase than to diminish. From the yard gate we saw the unending columns of fighting men marching jauntily back to the railway stations, and we looked on as the tanks and guns and wagons rolled by on their way home. But we were left where we were. Like the other men, Albert was becoming impatient. Like them he wanted only to get back home as quickly as possible.

Morning parade took place as usual every morning in the centre of the cobbled yard, followed by Major Martin's inspection of the horses and stables. But one dreary, drizzling morning, with the wet cobbles shining grey in the early morning light, Major Martin did not inspect the stables as usual. Sergeant 'Thunder' stood the men at ease and Major Martin announced the re-embarkation plans for the unit. He was finishing his short speech; 'So we shall be at Victoria Station by six

o'clock on Saturday evening—with any luck. Chances are you'll all be home by Christmas.'

'Permission to speak, sir?' Sergeant 'Thunder' ventured.

'Carry on, Sergeant.'

'It's about the 'orses, sir,' Sergeant 'Thunder' said. 'I think the men would like to know what's going to 'appen with the 'orses. Will they be with us on the same ship, sir? Or will they be coming along later?'

Major Martin shifted his feet and looked down at his boots. He spoke softly as if he did not want to be heard. 'No, Sergeant,' he said. 'I'm afraid the horses won't be coming with us at all.' There was an audible muttering of protest from the parading soldiers.

'You mean, sir,' said the sergeant. 'You mean that they'll be coming on a later ship?'

'No, Sergeant,' said the major, slapping his side with his swagger stick, 'I don't mean that. I mean exactly what I said. I mean they will not be coming with us at all. The horses will be staying in France.'

''Ere, sir?' said the sergeant. 'But 'ow can they, sir? Who'll be looking after them? We've got cases 'ere that need attention all day and every day.'

The major nodded, his eyes still looking at the ground. 'You'll not like what I have to tell you,' he said. 'I'm afraid a decision has been taken to sell off many of the army's horses here in France. All the horses we have here are either sick or have been sick. It's not considered worthwhile to transport them back home. My orders are to hold a horse sale here in this courtyard tomorrow morning. A notice has been posted in neighbouring towns to that effect. They are to be sold by auction.'

'Auctioned off, sir? Our 'orses to be put under the 'ammer, after all they've been through?' The sergeant

spoke politely, but only just. 'But you know what that means, sir? You know what will 'appen?'

'Yes, Sergeant,' said Major Martin. 'I know what will happen to them. But there's nothing anyone can do. We're in the army, Sergeant, and I don't have to remind you that orders are orders.'

'But you know what they'll go for,' said Sergeant 'Thunder', barely disguising the disgust in his voice. 'There's thousands of our 'orses out 'ere in France, sir. War veterans they are. D'you mean to say that after all they've been through, after all we've done lookin' after 'em, after all you've done, sir—that they're to end up like that? I can't believe they mean it, sir.'

'Well, I'm afraid they do,' said the major stiffly. 'Some of them may end up as you suggest—I can't deny it, Sergeant. You've every right to be indignant, every right. I'm not too happy about it myself, as you can imagine. But by tomorrow most of these horses will have been sold off, and we shall be moving out ourselves the day after. And you know, Sergeant, and I know, there's not a blind thing I can do about it.'

Albert's voice rang out across the yard. 'What, all of them, sir? Every one of them? Even Joey that we brought back from the dead? Even him?'

Major Martin said nothing, but turned on his heel and walked away.

There was an air of determined conspiracy abroad in the yard that day. Whispering groups of men in dripping greatcoats, their collars turned up to keep the rain from their necks, huddled together, their voices low and earnest. Albert seemed scarcely to notice me all day. He would neither talk to me nor even look at me

but hurried through the daily routine of mucking out, haying up and grooming, in a deep and gloomy silence. I knew, as every horse in the yard knew, that we were threatened. I was torn with anxiety.

An ominous shadow had fallen on the yard that morning and not one of us could settle in our stables. When we were led out for exercise, we were jumpy and skittish and Albert, like the other soldiers, responded with impatience, jerking sharply at my halter, something I had never known him do before.

That evening the men were still talking but now Sergeant 'Thunder' was with them and they all stood together in the darkening yard. I could just see in the last of the evening light the glint of money in their hands. Sergeant 'Thunder' carried a small tin box which was being passed around from one to the other and I heard the clink of coins as they were dropped in. The rain had stopped now and it was a still evening so that I could just make out Sergeant 'Thunder's' low, growling voice.

'That's the best we can do, lads,' he was saying. 'It's not a lot, but then we 'aven't got a lot, 'ave we? No one ever gets rich in this man's army. I'll do the bidding like I said—it's against orders, but I'll do it. Mind you, I'm not promising anything.' He paused and looked over his shoulder before going on. 'I'm not supposed to tell you this—the major said not to—and make no mistake, I'm not in the 'abit of disobeying officers' orders. But we aren't at war any more, and anyway this order was more like advice, so to speak. So I'm telling you this cos I wouldn't like you to think badly of the major. 'E knows what's going on right enough. Matter of fact the 'ole thing was 'is own idea. It was 'im that told me to suggest it to you in the first place. What's more, lads, 'e's given us every penny of 'is pay that 'e

'ad saved up—every penny. It's not much but it'll 'elp. 'Course I don't 'ave to tell you that no one says a word about this, not a dicky bird. If this was to get about, then 'e goes for the 'igh jump, like all of us would. So Mum's the word, clear?'

'Have you got enough, Sarge?' I could hear that it was Albert's voice speaking.

'I'm 'oping so, son,' Sergeant 'Thunder' said, shaking the tin. 'I'm 'oping so. Now let's all of us get some shut-eye. I want you layabouts up bright and early in the morning and them 'orses looking their thundering best. It's the last thing we'll be doing for 'em, least we can do for 'em seems to me.'

And so the group dispersed, the men walking away in twos and threes, shoulders hunched against the cold, their hands deep in their greatcoat pockets. One man only was left standing by himself in the yard. He stood for a moment looking up at the sky before walking over towards my stable. I could tell it was Albert from the way he walked—it was that rolling farmer's gait with the knees never quite straightening up after each stride.

He pushed back his peaked cap as he leant over the stable door. 'I've done all I can, Joey,' he said. 'We all have. I can't tell you any more cos I know you'd understand every word I said, and then you'd only worry yourself sick with it. This time, Joey, I can't even make you a promise like I did when Father sold you off to the army. I can't make you a promise cos I don't know whether I can keep it. I asked old "Thunder" to help and he helped. I asked the major to help and he helped. And now I've just asked God, cos when all's said and done, it's all up to him. We've done all we can, that's for certain sure. I remember old Miss Wirtle telling me in Sunday School back home once: "God helps those that helps themselves". Mean old

divil she was, but she knew her scriptures right enough. God bless you, Joey. Sleep tight.'

He put out his clenched fist and rubbed my muzzle, and then stroked each of my ears in turn before leaving me alone in the dark of the stables.

The day dawned bright over the clock tower, throwing the long, lean shadows of the poplars beyond across the cobbles that glistened with frost. Albert was up with the others before reveille was blown, so that by the time the first buyers arrived in the yard in their carts and cars, I was fed and watered and groomed so hard that my winter coat gleamed red as I was led out into the morning sun.

The buyers were gathered in the middle of the yard, and we were led, all those that could walk, around the perimeter of the yard in a grand parade, before being brought out one by one to face the auctioneer and the buyers. I found myself waiting in my stable watching every horse in the yard being sold ahead of me. I was, it seemed, to be the last to be brought out. Distant echoes of an earlier auction sent me suddenly into a feverish sweat, but I forced myself to remember Albert's reassuring words of the night before, and in time my heart stopped racing.

When Albert led me out into the yard I was calm and easy in my stride. I had unswerving faith in him as he patted my neck gently and whispered secretly in my ear. There were audible and visible signs of approval from the buyers as he walked me round in a tight circle, bringing me at last to a standstill facing a line of red, craggy faces and grasping, greedy eyes. Then I noticed in amongst the shabby coats and hats of the buyers, the still, tall figure of Sergeant 'Thunder' towering above them, and to one side the entire veterinary unit lined up along the wall and

watching the proceedings anxiously. The bidding began.

I was clearly much in demand for the bidding was swift to start with, but as the price rose I could see more heads shaking and very soon there seemed to be only two bidders left. One was old 'Thunder' himself, who would touch the corner of his cap with his stick, almost like a salute, to make his bid; and the other was a thin, wiry little man with weasel eyes who wore on his face a smile so full of consummate greed and evil that I could hardly bear to look at him. Still the price moved up

'At twenty-five, twenty-six. At twenty-seven. Twenty-seven I'm bid. On my right. Twenty-seven I'm bid. Any more please? It's against the sergeant there, at twenty-seven. Any more, please? He's a fine young animal, as you see. Got to be worth a lot more than this. Any more, please?' But the sergeant was shaking his head now, his eyes looked down and acknowledged defeat.

'Oh God, no,' I heard Albert whisper beside me. 'Dear God, not him. He's one of them, Joey. He's been buying all morning. Old "Thunder" says he's the butcher from Cambrai. Please God, no.'

'Well then, if there are no more bids, I'm selling to Monsieur Cirac of Cambrai at twenty-seven English pounds. Is that all? Selling then for twenty-seven. Going, going . . . '

'Twenty-eight,' came a voice from amongst the buyers, and I saw a white haired old man leaning heavily on his stick, shuffle slowly forward through the buyers until he stood in front of them. 'I'm bidding you twenty-eight of your English pounds,' said the old man, speaking in hesitant English. 'And I'll bid for so long and so high as I need to, I advise you, sir,' he

said, turning to the butcher from Cambrai. 'I advise you not to try to bid me out. For this horse I will pay one hundred English pounds if I must do. No one will have this horse except me. This is my Emilie's horse. It is hers by right.'

Before he spoke her name I had not been quite sure that my eyes and ears were not deceiving me, for the old man had aged many years since I had last set eyes on him, and his voice was thinner and weaker than I remembered. But now I was sure. This was indeed Emilie's grandfather standing before me, his mouth set with grim determination, his eyes glaring around him, challenging anyone to try to outbid him. No one said a word. The butcher from Cambrai shook his head and turned away. Even the auctioneer had been stunned into silence, and there was some delay before he brought his hammer down on the table and I was sold.

There was a look of resigned dejection on Sergeant 'Thunder's' face as he and Major Martin spoke together with Emilie's grandfather after the sale. The yard was empty now of horses and the buyers were all driving away. Albert and his friends stood around me commiserating with each other, all of them trying to comfort Albert. 'No need to worry, Albert,' one of them was saying. 'After all, could have been worse, couldn't it? I mean, a lot more'n half of our horses have gone to the butchers and that's for definite. At least we know Joey's safe enough with that old farmer man.'

'How do you know that?' Albert asked. 'How do you know he's a farmer?'

'I heard him telling old "Thunder", didn't I? Heard him saying he's got a farm down in the valley. Told old "Thunder" that Joey would never have to work again

so long as he lived. Kept rabbiting on about a girl called Emilie or something. Couldn't understand half of what he was saying.'

'Dunno what to make of him,' said Albert. 'Sounds mad as a hatter, the way he goes on. "Emilie's horse by right"—whoever she may be—isn't that what the old man said? What the divil did he mean by that? If Joey belongs to anyone by right, then he belongs to the army, and if he doesn't belong to the army, he belongs to me.'

'Better ask him yourself, Albert,' said someone else. 'Here's your chance. He's coming over this way with the major and old "Thunder".'

Albert stood with his arm under my chin, his hand reaching up to scratch me behind my ear, just where he knew I liked it best. As the major came closer though, he took his hand away, came to attention and saluted smartly. 'Begging your pardon, sir,' he said. 'I'd like to thank you for what you did, sir. I know what you did, sir, and I'm grateful. Not your fault we didn't quite make it, but thanks all the same, sir.'

'I don't know what he's talking about,' said Major Martin. 'Do you, Sergeant?'

'Can't imagine, sir,' said Sergeant 'Thunder'. 'They get like that you know, sir, these farming lads. It's cos they're brung up on cider instead of milk. It's true, sir, goes to their 'eads, sir. Must do, mustn't it?'

'Begging your pardon, sir,' Albert went on, puzzled by their levity. 'I'd like to ask the Frenchman, sir, since he's gone and bought my Joey. I'd like to ask him about what he said, sir, about this Emilie, or whatever she was called.'

'It's a long story,' said Major Martin, and he turned to the old man. 'Perhaps you would like to tell him yourself, Monsieur? This is the young man we were

speaking of, Monsieur, the one who grew up with the horse and who came all the way to France just to look for him.'

Emilie's grandfather stood looking sternly up at my Albert from under his bushy white eyebrows, and then his face cracked suddenly and he held out his hand and smiled. Although surprised, Albert reached and shook his hand. 'So, young man. We have much in common you and I. I am French and you are Tommy. True, I am old and you are young. But we share a love for this horse, do we not? And I am told by the officer here that at home in England you are a farmer, like I am. It is the best thing to be, and I say that with the wisdom of years behind me. What do you keep on your farm?'

'Sheep, sir, mostly. A few beef cattle and some pigs,' said Albert. 'Plough a few fields of barley as well.'

'So, it was you that trained the horse to be a farm horse?' said the old man. 'You did well, my son, very well. I can see the question in your eyes before you ask it, so I'll tell you how I know. You see your horse and I are old friends. He came to live with us—oh it was a long time ago now, not long after the war began. He was captured by the Germans and they used him for pulling their ambulance cart from the hospital to the front line and back again. There was with him another wonderful horse, a great shining black horse, and the two of them came to live in our farm that was near the German Field Hospital. My little grand-daughter, Emilie, cared for them and came to love them like her own family. I was all the family she had left—the war had taken the rest. The horses lived with us for maybe a year, maybe less, maybe more—it does not matter. The Germans were kind and gave us the horses when they left, and so they became ours, Emilie's and mine.

'Then one day they came back, different Germans, not kind like the others; they needed horses for their guns and so they took our horses away with them when they left. There was nothing I could do. After that my Emilie lost the will to live. She was a sick child anyway, but now with her family dead and her new family taken from her, she no longer had anything to live for. She just faded away and died last year. She was only fifteen years old. But before she died she made me promise her that I would find the horses somehow and look after them. I have been to many horse sales, but I have never found the other one, the black one. But now at last I have found one of them to take home and care for as I promised my Emilie.'

He leant more heavily on his stick now with both hands. He spoke slowly, choosing his words carefully. 'Tommy,' he went on. 'You are a farmer, a British farmer and you will understand that a farmer, whether he is British or French—even a Belgian farmer—never gives things away. He can never afford to. We have to live, do we not? Your major and your sergeant have told me how much you love this horse. They told me how every one of these men tried so hard to buy this horse. I think that is a noble thing. I think my Emilie would have liked that. I think she would understand, that she would want me to do what I will do now. I am an old man. What would I do with my Emilie's horse? He cannot grow fat in a field all his life, and soon I will be too old to look after him anyway. And if I remember him well, and I do, he loves to work, does he not? I have—how you say?—a proposition to make to you. I will sell my Emilie's horse to you.'

'Sell?' said Albert. 'But I cannot pay you enough to buy him. You must know that. We collected only twenty-six pounds between us and you paid

twenty-eight pounds. How can I afford to buy him from you?'

'You do not understand, my friend,' the old man said, suppressing a chuckle. 'You do not understand at all. I will sell you this horse for one English penny, *and* for a solemn promise—that you will always love this horse as much as my Emilie did and that you will care for him until the end of his days; and more than this, I want you to tell everyone about my Emilie and about how she looked after your Joey and the great black horse when they came to live with us. You see, my friend, I want my Emilie to live on in people's hearts. I shall die soon, in a few years, no more; and then no one will remember my Emilie as she was. I have no other family left alive to remember her. She will be just a name on a gravestone that no one will read. So I want you to tell your friends at home about my Emilie. Otherwise it will be as if she had never even lived. Will you do this for me? That way she will live for ever and that is what I want. Is it a bargain between us?'

Albert said nothing for he was too moved to speak. He simply held out his hand in acceptance; but the old man ignored it, put his hands on Albert's shoulders and kissed him on both cheeks. 'Thank you,' he said. And then he turned and shook hands with every soldier in the Unit and at last hobbled back and stood in front of me. 'Goodbye, my friend,' he said, and he touched me lightly on my nose with his lips. 'From Emilie,' he said, and then walked away. He had gone only a few paces before he stopped and turned around. Wagging his knobbly stick and with a mocking, accusing grin across his face, he said, 'Then it is true what we say, that there is only one thing at which the English are better than the French. They are meaner. You have not paid me my English penny, my friend.' Sergeant 'Thunder'

produced a penny from the tin and gave it to Albert, who ran over to Emilie's grandfather.

'I shall treasure it,' said the old man. 'I shall treasure it always.'

OBE

I know a Captain of Industry,
Who made big bombs for the RFC,
And collared a lot of £ s. d.—
And he—thank God!—has the OBE.

I know a Lady of Pedigree,
Who asked some soldiers out to tea,
And said 'Dear me!' and 'Yes, I see'—
And she—thank God!—has the OBE.

I know a fellow of twenty-three,
Who got a job with a fat MP—
(Not caring much for the Infantry.)
And he—thank God!—has the OBE.

I had a friend; a friend, and he
Just held the line for you and me,
And kept the Germans from the sea,
And died—without the OBE.
Thank God!
He died without the OBE.

A. A. Milne

The English children's writer A. A. Milne (1882–1956) is best known for his *Winnie the Pooh* stories and verse (*When We Were Very Young* and *Now We Are Six*). But he, like many other writers, was affected by the dreadful suffering of World War I, and wrote this bitter poem against those who gained the award of an OBE (Order of the British Empire), yet were far from the war action.

from *I Am David*

ANNE HOLM

The Danish children's writer Anne Holm first published her moving story in Denmark in 1963. It came out in English two years later. The story concerns a twelve-year-old Jewish boy, David, who is determined to escape from Nazi-occupied Greece, via the port of Salonica, to Italy, and then all the way to Denmark. If caught he will certainly be put in a concentration camp and probably killed.

David lay quite still in the darkness, listening to the men's low muttering. But this evening he was aware of their voices only as a vague meaningless noise in the distance, and he paid no attention to what they were saying.

'You must get away tonight,' the man had told him. 'Stay awake so that you're ready just before the guard's changed. When you see me strike a match, the current will be cut off and you can climb over—you'll have half a minute for it, no more.'

In his mind's eye David saw once again the grey

bare room he knew so well. He saw the man and was conscious, somewhere in the pit of his stomach, of the hard knot of hate he felt whenever he saw him. The man's eyes were small, repulsive, light in colour, their expression never changing; his face was gross and fat. David had known him all his life, but he never spoke to him more than was barely necessary to answer his questions; and though he had known his name for as long as he could remember, he never said anything but 'the man' when he spoke about him or thought of him. Giving him a name would be like admitting that he knew him; it would place him on an equal footing with the others.

But that evening he had spoken to him. He had said, 'And if I don't escape?'

The man had shrugged his shoulders. 'That'll be none of my business. I have to leave here tomorrow, and whatever my successor may decide to do about you, I shan't be able to interfere. But you'll soon be a big lad, and there's need in a good many places for those strong enough to work.'

David knew only too well that those other places would not be any better than the camp where he now was. 'And if I get away without being caught, what then?' he had asked.

'Just by the big tree in the thicket that lies on the road out to the mines, you'll find a bottle of water and a compass. Follow the compass southwards till you get to Salonica, and then when no one's looking go on board a ship and hide. You'll have to stay hidden while the ship's at sea, and you'll need the water. Find a ship that's bound for Italy, and when you get there go north till you come to a country called Denmark—you'll be safe there.'

David had very nearly shown his astonishment, but

he controlled himself, and hiding his feelings merely said, 'I don't know what a compass is.'

The man had shown him one, telling him that the four letters indicated north, south, east, and west, and that the needle, which swung freely, always pointed in the same direction. Then he had added, 'The half minute the current's cut off is intended for you. If you try to take anyone with you, you can be sure that neither of you will get away. And now clear off before you're missed.'

David did not know what possessed him to say it—he had never asked the man for anything, partly because he knew it would be of no use, but chiefly because he would not—when you hated someone, you did not ask him for anything. But tonight he had done it: when he reached the door, he turned round, and looking straight into that coarse heavy face said, 'I'd like a piece of soap.'

For a moment there had been complete silence in that bare grey room. Then the man picked up a cake of soap that lay by the side of the wash-basin in the corner and threw it on the table. All he said was, 'Now go.'

So David had gone, as quickly as it was possible to go without appearing to be in a hurry.

The men's muttering was fainter now—some of them must have fallen asleep. The camp's latest arrival was still talking. David recognized his voice because it was less flat and grating than the others. Whenever the newcomer dozed off to sleep, he was seized with a nightmare, and then they would all wake up again. The night before, this had happened just before the guard was changed, but if he took longer to fall asleep this evening, then it might be possible for David to slip out before the others were wakened again.

David was not yet sure whether he would make the attempt. He tried to work out why the man had told him to do it. It was certainly a trap: just as he was climbing over, the searchlight would suddenly swing round and catch him in its beam, and then they would shoot. Perhaps something pleasant was going to happen tomorrow and the man wanted him shot first. David had always known that the man hated him, just as much as David hated *him* in return. On the other hand, nothing pleasant had ever yet happened in the camp that David could remember, and he was now twelve years old—it said so on his identity-card.

And then quite suddenly David decided he would do it. He had turned it over in his mind until his head was in a whirl and he still could not understand why the man had told him to escape. Suppose it were a trap and they shot him, it would all be over quickly anyway. If you were fired at while trying to escape, you would be dead within a minute. Yes, David decided to try.

There could not be many minutes left now. Over in the guard-room he could hear them moving about and getting dressed, and he could hear the guard yawning as his pace grew slower. Then came the sound of new steps and David pressed himself even more closely against the wall. It was the man; the faint sleepy yellow light from the guard-room shone for a moment on his face as he passed the window. He went up to the guard, and David suddenly felt quite empty inside and was sure that he would be unable to move when the time came. Then he saw before him the endless succession of days, months, and years that would pass if he did not. The waiting would kill him in the end, but it might take years. And it would grow worse and worse,

all the time: David clenched his teeth so hard that he felt the muscles of his throat grow taut. Then the man struck a match.

Nineteen, twenty . . . the half minute would be up when he had counted slowly to thirty . . . David set his foot in a gap higher up the barbed wire . . . When would the searchlight come? They could not be certain of hitting him in the dark . . . and if they did not hurry he would be over.

A moment later he had touched the ground on the other side, and as he ran he said angrily to himself, 'What a fool you are! There's plenty of ground to cover yet—all this great flat stretch without so much as the stump of a tree for shelter. They'll wait till you've nearly reached the thicket . . . they'll think it more amusing if you believe you've almost got to safety.'

Why didn't they hurry up? The thought pounded through his head as every moment he expected to see the ground lit up in front of him. Then he stopped. He would run no more. When the beam of light caught him, they should see him walking away quite calmly. Then they would not enjoy it so much, they would feel cheated. The thought filled David with triumph.

When he was little, it had been his most burning desire to get the better of them, especially of the man. And now he would! They would be forced to shoot him as they watched him walking quietly away and taking no notice of them!

David was so taken up with his victory over them that he had gone a dozen yards past the spot where the thicket hid him from the camp before he realized that no one had fired. He stopped short. What could have happened? He turned, found a place where the thicket was thin enough to peer through and looked across at the low buildings outlined against the dark sky, like an

even darker smudge of blackness. He could faintly hear the tread of the guard, but it came no nearer and sounded no different from usual, only farther off. Nothing at all appeared different.

David frowned in the darkness and stood for a moment undecided: it couldn't possibly . . . ? He trotted on, following the edge of the thicket towards the big tree, running faster the nearer he got, and when he reached the tree he threw himself down on the ground, searching frantically with his hands round the trunk.

There was the bundle. David leaned up against the tree shivering with cold although it was not cold at all. The bundle was a piece of cloth wrapped round something and tied in a knot. He fumbled with the knot but his fingers were clumsy and would not respond—and then he suddenly realized that he dared not undo it. There would be something dangerous inside the bundle . . . He tried to gather his thoughts together sufficiently to think what it might be, but his imagination did not get beyond a bomb.

It would make little difference, he thought desperately—a bullet or a bomb: it would soon be over, either way. Frantically, his fingers awkward, he struggled with the knot.

But there was no bomb in the cloth. It was a square handkerchief tied cross-wise over a bottle of water and a compass, just as the man had said. He barely managed to turn aside before he was sick.

Afterwards he felt carefully all round the square-shaped bundle. A bottle, a compass—there was something else. David's eyes had grown accustomed to the darkness: in the bundle there were also a box of matches, a large loaf of bread, and a pocket-knife.

So the man had intended him to escape after all! A search-party would be sent out for him in the morning,

but not before. The night was his, and it was up to him to make the most of it.

All this had taken only a few minutes, but to David it felt like hours. His hand closed tightly round the soap—he had not let go of it for a moment since he first got it. He recalled the hours he had spent that evening lying on his plank-bed listening to the muttered conversation of the men and thinking over what the man had said. He remembered, too, that it would be only a matter of time before he was caught again; but that, like everything else, no longer seemed important. All that mattered now was his bundle and the freedom of the night that lay ahead. Slowly he tucked the piece of soap into a corner of the handkerchief, laid the bottle, bread, and knife on top, tied the ends together, took a firm grip on the knot and looked at the compass in his hand.

Then he ran.

When he looked back afterwards, all he could recall of the five days that followed was running and looking all the time at the compass to make sure he was travelling in the right direction. Every night he ran, and he ran all night long. Once he slipped into a water-hole and the mud caked on him as it dried. Once he was so torn by branches that blood oozed from the scratches on his face, hands, and legs. He would never forget that night. He had come to a close thicket of thorn bushes, and the needle indicated that he should go straight through it. He had hesitated a moment and then tried running a few yards along the edge of it, but the compass needle immediately swung round. Perhaps he could have recovered his direction a little farther on, but he knew so little about compasses that he dared not risk it. And

so he plunged into the thicket, elbows up to protect his face. The first branch that struck him hurt painfully, and so did the first gash along his arm, but after that he noticed nothing and just crashed his way through. The nights were usually completely quiet, but that night he could hear a whimpering moan the whole time. Not until afterwards did he realize that the sound had come from himself.

He ran all the time, sometimes fairly slowly so that it took him hours to go a short way, sometimes so quickly that he felt his blood pounding. Every morning with the first glimmer of daylight he lay down to sleep. It was not very difficult to find somewhere to sleep in that sparsely inhabited district. David had no idea what the countryside looked like: for him it was only a place where he must run through the night and hide by day.

Two other incidents remained in his memory: they were moments when fear grew to a sharp-pointed terror that seemed to pierce him right through. The first happened just as it was growing dark one evening. David was awakened by something warm and hairy touching his hand. He lay still, tense with fear. It was some minutes before he could bring himself to turn his head, and then he saw—a sheep.

But it spelled danger, nevertheless, for where there are sheep there must also be people, and that evening David did not stop to recover his breath for some hours afterwards.

Yet he was glad enough to come across more sheep later that night. David was used to hard work and satisfied with very little food, and he had been as sparing as he could with the bread and water, but after two whole days the bottle was empty and the bread eaten. He could manage without bread but it was dreadful to be so thirsty. In the end he could think of

hardly anything but water. But where was he to get it?

At that point he almost stumbled over two shepherds who lay asleep on the ground wrapped in their cloaks. His heart, which had been thumping so loudly all through the night, missed a beat, so terror-stricken was he. But he stopped himself just in time: bare feet make no noise and the two men had heard nothing.

David was about to step back, slowly and cautiously, when he caught sight, in the moonlight, of a bucket with a lid and the embers of a burned-down fire. Food! And where there was food, there was probably water, too!

That night David went no further. He kept watch till daybreak, far enough off to give him a chance to escape should that prove necessary, and yet near enough to be back in a moment as soon as the two shepherds were out of sight in the morning. There was little doubt that this was their regular camping-place for the night, for they left their bundles and the bucket behind. Perhaps they would soon be back, but that was a risk David decided he must take. Without food, or at least without water, he would not be able to last many more hours. He was familiar enough from his experiences in the camp with what happened when a man was left without food and water.

What had nearly proved a catastrophe ended as a stroke of good fortune. There was some soup left in the bucket, and in one of the bundles he found a chunk of bread. He broke the bread unevenly, leaving a small piece behind, and then filling his bottle with soup he replaced the lid and knocked it off again with his elbow. He did not know whether sheep ate bread and soup, but he wanted to make it look as if they had been there.

After that night he took care to run at a more even pace and to stop more often, but for shorter periods, to recover his breath. He must not again risk being so tired that he saw nothing and stumbled on blindly.

David edged cautiously forward on his stomach. It was the second time he had found himself close to a town, and for the second time the compass was directing him to cross a main road. He dared not disobey it; it was almost as if some part of the man himself were travelling with him.

He ought to have asked how long it would take him to reach Salonica. He had only two mouthfuls of soup left now and a single bite of bread.

And there were people about. That meant he had not nearly so much of the night at his disposal—he would have to wait until they had gone to bed. He told himself that he should have known all along that he would occasionally come across towns . . . He forced himself to lie absolutely still.

But he was not sleepy any longer, and when he was not sleepy lying still became almost unbearable, for then it was difficult not to think—and David knew that he must not think. He had learned that—then. The only thing to do was to take no notice: you could look and listen, but you must not let what you heard or saw penetrate your thoughts. You must not let your thoughts dwell upon anything more important than whether it would rain or turn out fine, whether you had long to wait for your next meal, or how long it would be till the guard was changed. And you must not be too interested in those things either—you must merely make use of them to fill your thoughts and prevent other things from slipping into your mind.

Since the evening of his escape, the things that had formerly occupied his thoughts were no longer there, and others had taken their place. He gave his mind to hurrying along as fast as possible during the night, to stopping as soon as the darkness began to lift so that he could find a good hiding-place before day broke, to looking after his bundle and avoiding the temptation of taking an extra bite or another drop to drink, to going in the right direction all the time so that the compass needle did not shift its position. These things served to fill his thoughts to the exclusion of other matters. But when it came to lying still and yet being wide awake—that was dangerous! So he began to think about a feeling he had had several times during the previous night—that the ground he was travelling over was changing, becoming more up-and-down . . . that mountains would bar the road to Salonica.

Don't think, don't think! David clenched his hands, gripping a tuft of grass. He mustn't think at all, for if he did, there was only one thing to think about—that he would not be able to run any further. Why had they not caught him the night he crossed the bridge? He could not swim, so the bridge had been his only way over the river, and he had been quite sure he would be caught there. Yes, that had been the only restful moment in all those long days and nights—crossing that bridge and feeling certain they would catch him.

But no one had come.

A Fight to a Finish

'Fight the year out!' the War-lords said:
What said the dying among the dead?

'To the last man!' cried the profiteers:
What said the poor in the starveling years?

'War is good!' yelled the Jingo-kind:
What said the wounded, the maimed, and blind?

'Fight on!' the Armament-kings besought:
Nobody asked what the women thought.

S. Gertrude Ford

from *Friedrich*

HANS PETER RICHTER

Translated by Edita Kroll

Hans Peter Richter was born in Cologne, Germany, between the two World Wars. He has written over twenty books for children, one of his first being *Friedrich* in 1961: *Damals War Es Friedrich*—'There was Once Friedrich'. It came out in English in 1970.

The story is told by a German boy living in the same house as Friedrich, a Jewish boy in hiding in Germany during World War II. His father (Herr Schneider) is arrested one day while Friedrich is out—given away, along with a rabbi, a Jewish religious leader, by the house landlord, Herr Resch. As the story shows, not all Germans were against the Jews; some did what they could to help save them from the Nazis.

It was quite dark on the stairs. Softly, I knocked the arranged signal: once—long pause—twice—short pause—three times.

Inside I heard cautious noises. Someone opened the door. It stayed dark. A hand slid along the door frame;

the lock cracked; a small black gap between frame and door slowly grew wider.

The door only opened all the way after I had whispered my name three times. I slipped inside and waited in the pitch-dark hall until the door had been closed again, equally gently.

A hand touched my arm, held it and pulled me along.

I recognized the grip; it was the rabbi.

We crept to the living room.

The rabbi scratched at the door. Then he pushed it open.

There was no light in the living room, either. The rabbi lit a single candle only after we stood inside the room.

The living room had a grim, hopeless look. Every window was thickly covered. By the light spots on the walls one could still make out where the furniture had stood. On the floor lay a pallet of old blankets, mattresses, and rags. The table in the centre of the room seemed the only usable piece of furniture left. And on the table, in all its splendour, sat the candle in its silver Sabbath holder.

'Where is Friedrich?' I asked.

Sitting at the table, Herr Schneider shrugged his shoulders. 'Gone to see friends!' he answered. 'Curfew must have surprised him there. He'll probably stay there till morning.'

The rabbi had sat down. He picked up an old coat from the floor. 'You have better eyes than I. Could you please thread this needle for me?' He handed me a needle and a piece of black thread.

While I tried to thread the needle, the rabbi explained: 'It's time again, you see. Once more we must wear a yellow star.' He pointed to a pile of yellow stars on the table.

The yellow stars with black rims, the size of saucers, had to be fastened over the left breast. They were formed like stars of David. The word 'Jew' was woven in the centre, in letters resembling Hebrew.

Herr Schneider got up. He bowed to me as if on a stage. Then he undid the knot of his scarf and hung it over the chair. With his left hand he pointed to his left side. On his coat was a yellow star!

He unbuttoned his coat. On his jacket was a yellow star! He opened his jacket. On his waistcoat a yellow star! 'In the old days Jews had to wear pointed yellow hats!' His voice was mocking. 'This time it's yellow stars—we've gone back to the Middle Ages!'

'And soon,' the rabbi added, 'soon they'll perhaps burn us, as in the Middle Ages!'

'But why?' I asked.

'Why?' the rabbi repeated softly. 'Why? It's decided in heaven who gets raised and who gets humbled. The Lord our God, His Name be praised, has chosen us among all peoples. Because we are different, just because we are different, we are persecuted and killed.'

. . .

We were already in bed when we heard the noise downstairs.

Several men were climbing the stairs to the third floor. They rang the bell. When no one opened the door, they pummelled it with their fists, shouting: 'Open up at once! Police!'

Nothing moved in the Schneiders' apartment.

Father and Mother threw on coats and went as far as our hall. Trembling, we listened behind our door.

'Just a moment, please!' we heard Herr Resch say downstairs. 'Don't break down the door! I have a

second key! I'll open it for you!' Gasping for air, he dragged himself upstairs.

'That pig!' said my father.

Upstairs we heard the door being unlocked. With a crash it flew against the wall. 'Hands up!' shouted a voice.

Then it grew still again. Only heavy footsteps sounded above our heads.

'Let's go outside,' Father ordered. The three of us went and stood on the landing.

Shortly thereafter a man wearing a helmet and a trench coat came down the stairs. 'Out of the way! Scram!' he snarled when he saw us.

Father took hold of Mother's and my arms. We stayed where we were.

Then came the rabbi. They had put him in handcuffs. A young man pulled him along, smiling at us. The rabbi looked first at Father, then at me, before lowering his head.

Herr Schneider came last. A small man in jackboots accompanied him, holding onto his handcuffs.

When Herr Schneider saw my father he said in a loud voice, 'You were right, Herr . . . '

A blow from the fist of the little man cut off the sentence; the little man had hit so hard that Herr Schneider reeled under the impact.

Herr Schneider said no more. Blood ran from his lower lip. Once more he looked at us all, lifted his shoulders in resignation, and let himself be dragged along by the little man.

Upstairs the door was being locked.

'One is missing!' Herr Resch screeched. 'You forgot one!'

'Shut your mouth!' ordered a clear voice. It belonged to a slim man who was running down the

stairs. He held a red folder in his hand. When he noticed us on the landing, he indicated our door with his thumb and said, 'Get lost!'

After they had gone, Herr Resch made his groaning way downstairs, clad only in pyjamas. He was smiling and, rubbing his hands gleefully, said to Father: 'Finally got rid of that irksome tenant! And they caught a pretty bird on top of it!'

Father turned his back on him; pushing us inside the apartment, he flung the door shut so that its glass panes jingled.

No one slept that night. Father rolled restlessly from side to side, Mother wept, and I thought about Herr Schneider. Though none of us had to go out in the morning, everyone got up very early.

'We must intercept Friedrich when he gets home!' said Mother. 'He mustn't even enter their apartment.'

Father agreed. 'We must prepare him.'

Mother couldn't eat any breakfast.

Father drank only a little coffee.

I had to sit behind our door and watch. Breakfast was brought to me there. While I chewed, I kept listening to the noises on the stairs.

There were lots of them this morning. Doors banged; I heard footsteps. But they weren't Friedrich's. I knew his step.

After I had finished my breakfast I stacked the dishes and carried them to the kitchen.

At that very moment Friedrich raced up the stairs.

'Friedrich!' whispered Mother, her eyes full of horror.

Nervously I looked for a place to put down the dishes, finally pushing them into Mother's hands.

'Run!' she said, out of breath.

I ran up the stairs. Friedrich was nowhere to be seen.

The door stood open.

I went inside.

Friedrich was in the living room, barring the door with his legs spread wide. Motionless, he stared at Herr Resch.

Herr Resch was kneeling on the floor; his face, pale with fright, was turned towards him. His right hand was stuck inside the mattress; he held his left hand high to ward off Friedrich. He looked like a stone statue. Only his fingers trembled slightly.

Next to him lay Frau Resch's shopping bag. It was filled with Herr Schneider's books. Two lamps showed above the rim; one of the Schneiders' blankets hid the rest. The silver Sabbath holder could be seen because it wouldn't fit in the bag.

The floor was covered with papers, photos, letters. Someone had obviously searched through them and strewn them around.

One of the Schneiders' chests, filled with household things, stood by the door, ready for collection. Herr Schneider's little tool box lay on top.

There wasn't a sound to be heard.

In the street people were talking.

The stillness in the room was horrible.

A car went by outside.

My heart beat so loudly I thought I'd go mad. I didn't dare move.

The stillness seemed to have lasted forever, when Friedrich spat into Herr Resch's face. 'Vulture!' he screamed. 'Vulture!'

The spittle ran slowly down the face and over Herr Resch's mouth.

He wiped it off with his sleeve. He began to breathe in gasps. Blood came to his face, turning it red. His whole body began to shake. He grabbed for the Sabbath holder and missed. He reached for it a second time and got hold of it.

Friedrich still stood in the doorway, not moving a muscle.

Herr Resch pushed himself off the floor with difficulty. His breath whistling, he staggered towards Friedrich, the silver candleholder in his raised hand.

Friedrich held his ground.

'Help!' Herr Resch's voice rang through the house. 'I'm being attacked. Help!'

Friedrich turned calmly, taking his time. Then he saw me. I tried to signal to him.

'Jew!—Stop him!—Police!' screeched Herr Resch. Friedrich merely nodded, went by me and bounded down the stairs—out of the house—away.

. . .

The door to the public air-raid shelter was already locked. Father put down his suitcase and manoeuvred the iron bars. When the steel door still wouldn't budge, he hammered on it.

Herr Resch opened the door. He wore a steel helmet and an armband identifying him as the air-raid warden. 'About time, too!' he growled.

Father said nothing in reply.

We walked into the shelter, greeting everyone there with 'Heil Hitler!'

No one answered.

With eyes shut tight, women and old men sat spread over the room. Some had lain down on the benches. Everyone had his luggage beside him. Two mothers and their small children huddled in a dark corner. The

children were whining to themselves. In another corner, two lovers sat closely pressed against each other; the man was a sergeant.

We sat down close to the fresh-air pump—where we always sat. The luggage rested between our feet.

Father leaned against the dank, white wall and closed his eyes.

'You'll never get rid of that cough this way,' said Mother.

Father sat up straight. 'I can't sleep anyway,' he said.

'I believe you,' nodded Mother.

Herr Resch as air-raid warden crossed the shelter. 'Well, comrade, on leave?' he addressed the sergeant.

Startled, the sergeant shot up and agreed.

'We'll show them up there, eh?' Herr Resch was showing off. 'Did you read that we shot down thirty-five enemy bombers yesterday?'

The sergeant smiled. 'And thirty-five others are taking their places today, and God knows how many more will come!'

Herr Resch cleared his throat. Without another word, he turned and went back to the door.

The sergeant once more embraced his girl.

Outside the pounding grew louder, and the bark of our anti-aircraft guns sounded strangely hollow. The shots mingled with the sounds of bombs exploding, singly first, then several at once. Whole groups of bombs fell together. The cellar resounded with their explosions.

'The poor boy!' sighed Mother.

Father just said, 'Hmm.'

Herr Resch withdrew to the shelter proper, closing the airlock and making the shelter airtight.

Again a bomb exploded. This time, it hit so close the cellar walls shook under the impact.

Suddenly there came a pounding on the door.

'Who can that be so late?' muttered Herr Resch, searching the room.

'Well, go and open up!' the sergeant called from his corner.

Herr Resch unbarred the inner door. Now we could hear someone whimper outside. 'Please, please let me in. Please, pleeease!'

'Friedrich!' Mother burst out. Her mouth fell open, her eyes grew large.

'Open up! Open up!' the voice shouted, full of horror. 'Please, open up!'

Herr Resch opened the steel door.

Friedrich was kneeling outside, his hands folded in prayer. 'I am afraid. Afraid. Afraid.' On all fours, he crept into the airlock of the shelter.

Through the open door we could hear how hellish it was outside. The pressure of another hit threw the steel door shut.

'Out!' bellowed Herr Resch. 'Scram! You don't really imagine we'd let you into our shelter, do you?' His breathing was laboured. 'Out! Get out!'

The sergeant stood up and walked over to Herr Resch. 'Have you gone out of your mind? You can't send the boy out of a shelter in this raid!'

'Do you know who that is?' Herr Resch sputtered. 'That's a Jew!'

'So?' the sergeant asked with astonishment. 'And even if it were but a dog, you'd let him stay until the raid is over.'

The other people in the shelter also took part now. 'Let the boy stay!' came from all sides.

'Who do you think you are!' Herr Resch screamed. 'How dare you mix in my affairs? Who is air-raid warden here, you or I? You follow my orders, is that understood? Otherwise I'll report you.'

No longer sure of himself, the sergeant stood and looked at Friedrich. Everyone was silent. The guns still sounded.

Very pale, Friedrich still leaned in the airlock. He had calmed down.

'Go, boy. Go voluntarily!' the sergeant said softly. 'Otherwise there'll be nothing but annoyance.'

Without a word Friedrich left the shelter.

Shots and bombs thundered without a break. We could even hear the whistling sound of the falling bombs and the rushing sound of the incendiary bombs.

Mother cried against Father's shoulder.

'Do pull yourself together!' begged Father. 'You'll endanger us all otherwise.'

Dust and heat greeted us outside. The sky glowed red with the light of fires. Flames still came from roofs and hollow windows. Heaps of rubble smouldered. Glass splinters and fragments of tiles covered the street. In between lay the incendiary bombs that had missed their targets.

Desperate women cried in front of ruins from which clouds of dust and pulverized brick still rose. Beside a garden wall lay a human being. Someone had thrown a shredded slip over the face.

Supporting Mother between us, we searched for the way home.

Herr and Frau Resch came with us.

A bomb had ripped open the street outside our house, but the house still stood. The roof was partly uncovered and none of the windows had any glass.

We stepped into the front garden.

At once Herr Resch made for the little bit of lawn. He picked up his garden dwarf, Polycarp. A piece of

shrapnel had cut off the tip of his cap. Herr Resch searched for it. When he discovered it despite the darkness, he said to Father: 'What a shame! I'll try to glue it back on.'

Fearfully, Mother looked for Friedrich.

Friedrich sat in the shadow of the stoop. His eyes were closed, his face pale.

'Are you crazy?' Father couldn't help asking.

At that Herr Resch also noticed him.

Father was still standing on the path. It was obvious he didn't know what to do.

Herr Resch pushed his wife aside and stepped closer, still carrying Polycarp.

'Away from here!' he thundered at Friedrich. 'Do you think you no longer have to fear being sent away, just because everything's out of whack after this raid?'

Shrilly Mother said: 'Can't you see he's fainted!'

A mocking smile on his face, Herr Resch turned to Mother and said: 'Fainted indeed! I'll get him out of it quickly enough. But I must say I am surprised at your sympathy for a Jew. You, the wife of a member of the Nazi party.'

Father pulled her aside. She was sobbing.

Herr Resch lifted his foot and kicked.

Friedrich rolled out of the shelter entrance-way onto the stone path. A trail of blood went from his right temple to his collar.

I clutched the thorny rosebush.

'His luck that he died *this* way,' said Herr Resch.

At The Eastern Front

Like the wild organs of winter storms
Is a people's dark wrath,
The crimson wave of the battle,
Of leafless stars.

With broken brows, with silver arms,
To dying soldiers waves the night.
In the shades of the autumnal ash tree
Sigh the spirits of the slain.

Thorny wilderness strangles the town.
From bloodstained steps the moon
Harries the frightened women.
Wild wolves have broken through the gate.

Georg Trakl

Georg Trakl (1887–1914) joined the German Medical Corps at the start of World War I. After two months of war, at the age of 17, he committed suicide.

from *Hurricane Summer*

ROBERT SWINDELLS

This story of a young boy's experience of World War II in England is based partly on the author's own childhood memories in Yorkshire. The tale is seen through the eyes of Jim, a ten year old who has just lost his father, a sailor, in the war. The events of war merge with bullying at school, but Jim finds his own way of dealing with them.

Funny things, friendships. They tend to come and go, but most people have a special friend who stands out among all the others. I'm lucky—I've got two. One of them's been dead a long time now, but it doesn't matter—he'll always be my friend. As for the other . . . well, as I said, friendships are funny. Best thing I can do is tell you about them.

World War II was on and I was ten. I was an only child. My dad had been killed the previous autumn serving with the Navy. Mum said I must always remember that my dad had been a hero, and I knew he had, and that was the trouble.

You see, I wasn't a hero. Far from it.

There was this lad at school. Clive Simcox. He was the same age as me—we were in the same class—but Clive was taller and heavier and for some reason that summer he started picking on me. I didn't like fighting so I was forever trying to please him. I let him win at marbles and lent him my wicket keeper's gloves. I even gave him my best stamp—a Guadeloupe triangular—but it was no use. He'd still ambush me on the way home from school and bash me up. He used to wait for me in the mornings too, and trip me as I ran past. I'd arrive at school with grazed knees and dirt on my blazer and red eyes from crying, and everybody would know Clive had had another go at me.

He used to make remarks about my dad, which was even worse. Before the war Dad had been an electrician, so they made him an electrician in the Navy. I don't know what his work was exactly, but it had to do with electrical circuits and that sort of thing. Anyway, Simcox had latched on to this and sometimes he'd say, 'He was nothing special, you know, your dad. He wasn't a gunner or a torpedo man. He didn't kill any Germans. He was just an electrician, mending fuses and changing lightbulbs while other fellows did the fighting.' This would be in the playground or on the street and he'd say it at the top of his voice so everyone could hear, and all the time he'd be pushing me—shoving me in the chest so that I had to keep stepping backwards. He was goading me of course—trying to make me fight, but I was too scared. Red-faced with shame, I'd retreat till he got bored and went off to bother somebody else.

I despised myself. I'd think, what sort of kid doesn't stick up for his dead father? Defend his honour? If I was half the hero Dad was, I'd stand up to Simcox and

punch him on the nose, even if he bashed me up after. Sometimes, lying in bed in the morning I'd convince myself that this time I was going to do it. This time I'd turn with my fists up and give him the biggest surprise of his life, but I never did. When it came to it—when he was actually there in front of me with his red face and mocking eyes—I'd either try to run or let him hit me to get it over. I was ashamed of myself but I couldn't help it.

Funniest thing was, Simcox senior wasn't even in the forces. He worked in a button factory, but I daren't bring that up when Clive was tormenting me. Shows how scared I was, and believe me it's no joke being a coward when the world seems full of heroes.

Our world was full of heroes all right. The aerodrome was three times its pre-war size and three squadrons of Hurricanes were stationed there. Picton Hill, it was called. RAF Picton Hill. It's part of the industrial estate now, but in 1940 it was famous.

One hot afternoon, when I got in from school, I found Mum talking with one of these idols in the garden. I'd managed to dodge Clive for once, so I was fairly presentable. 'Jim,' smiled Mum, 'this is Pilot Officer Cochrane. He helped me home with my shopping.'

I was completely bowled over. Pilot Officer Cochrane really looked like a hero. Tall he was, and slim, with black hair and a tanned face. I'd never been close to a fighter pilot before, and when he stuck out his hand I stood gaping.

'Well, Jim?' laughed Mum. 'Aren't you going to shake hands?'

'Uh? Oh yes—sorry.' I shoved my paw out and he gripped it, grinning. His teeth were dazzlingly white. I

wondered fleetingly what he'd think if he knew he was shaking hands with a coward.

'Name's Mike,' he said, 'but my friends call me Cocky. I hope we're going to be friends, Jim.'

I could hardly believe it. A fighter pilot for a friend. They'd be green with envy at school. I looked at him. 'Do you spy a Flitfire—I mean, fly a Spitfire?'

He roared with laughter. Mum laughed too. I felt myself blushing.

'No,' he chuckled. 'I don't spy a Flitfire—I high a Flurricane.'

He stayed for tea. It was only sardines on toast, but I wished it could last for ever. He was really nice, and not a bit conceited. I was sure if I had wings on my tunic I'd be very conceited indeed.

One day we were flying the kite. It was a perfect day for it—breezy, with scudding clouds and sudden bursts of sunshine—but I couldn't stop thinking about Simcox and it was spoiling my day. Mum wasn't with us, so when we knocked off for the sandwiches and a flask of tea I decided to make a clean breast of it. 'Cocky,' I said, 'I wish I was fearless like you.'

He was winding the kite-string round the bit of dowelling we used for a handgrip. He laughed, glancing down at me. It was a short laugh, and there was no humour in it.

'Fearless?' He finished winding and handed me the kite. 'I'm not fearless, Jim. I'm petrified. Permanently petrified.'

I shook my head. I assumed he was joking. He was one of those people who can joke with a perfectly straight face.

'Oh yeah?' I grinned. 'Whoever heard of a petrified fighter pilot?'

'Nobody's heard, Jim,' he said. 'Everybody thinks we're fearless because that's what the newspapers say, but it's not true.' He sat down beside me, looking away towards the aerodrome. I put the kite down and started unwrapping the sandwiches.

After a minute he said, 'The papers have to say we're fearless to keep people's spirits up, but we're not. None of us.' He plucked a stalk of grass and chewed the end. He wasn't looking at me.

'Do you know what happens when a Hurricane catches fire, Jim?'

I shook my head. I'd seen planes come down in flames—we all had, but they were always a long way off.

Cocky went on gazing towards the aerodrome. 'What happens,' he said quietly, 'is that the fuel burns. Gallons and gallons of high-octane fuel. The slipstream blows the flames into the cockpit like a blowtorch, right into the pilot's face. If he gets out at once he might escape with blistered hands and cheeks. If he doesn't—and it usually takes a while to undo the harness and get the canopy off—those flames'll have destroyed his face and maybe his eyes as well. If he gets out then—if the pain hasn't caused him to faint and if the plane's not spinning, pinning him in the cockpit by centrifugal force—he's going to walk around for the rest of his life looking like something out of a horror story, even if he's not blind. He's going to catch people staring at him, then looking away quickly when they see he's noticed. He'll see people turn sick at the mere sight of him, and, of course, he's never going to kiss a pretty girl again.'

He turned his head to look at me. 'And you think

we're fearless, Jim? You think I'm not afraid?' He snorted. 'I've puked, laddie—got up out of my bed and thrown up at the mere thought of ever flying again. I'll tell you this, Jim. If I could—if I dared—I'd get up right now and start running, and I wouldn't stop till I was somewhere they'd never find me. And that's true of all fighter pilots—every one of us.' He sat up, wrapped his arms round his bony shins and rested his forehead on his knees. 'Only the insane are fearless, Jim. The rest of us carry on because we're trapped.'

I never did tell him about Simcox. I suppose his story made my problem seem piddling. It made me feel better though, knowing Cocky was afraid. Knowing I wasn't the only one. It certainly put paid to my illusions about the glamour of war.

One afternoon, just before the start of the summer holidays, I was helping Mum get the tea when there was a knock on the open door. We looked round and saw a pilot on the step. He didn't say anything. He just stood holding his cap in both hands, looking at Mum. Mum gazed back for a moment, then said in a quiet voice, 'It's Cocky, isn't it?'

The pilot nodded, stepping into the sunny kitchen. 'This morning,' he murmured, 'near Deal. I am most awfully sorry.' And Mum began to cry. I stared from one to the other till it sank in, then ran howling to my room.

I don't know if you've ever lost your best friend. I hope not. If you haven't, it's no use my trying to describe to you how I felt. You'd have to feel it for yourself. Anyway I was ill all night and Mum kept me off school next day, and in the middle of the morning there was an air raid.

The whole thing lasted about five minutes, then it went quiet, and after a bit the all clear sounded and I could hear the Hurricanes coming in to land.

I went back to bed. Half an hour later Mum came in. She'd been in the public shelter under the High Street.

'They hit a house,' she said, 'in Oasthouse Lane.' She said it in a flat, uninterested voice, and I knew she was grieving for Cocky.

Next day—it was Friday, the last day before the hols—I was trailing along the lane when suddenly Clive Simcox sprang out in front of me and snatched my cap. I don't know to this day what came over me, but before I knew what I was doing I'd clenched my fist and smashed it into the middle of Clive's face. He must've been really startled because he neither struck back nor covered up, but stood there gaping while blood ran from both nostrils into his mouth. I wanted to punch him again—to go on punching for all the times he'd bullied me, and for Dad, and Cocky, but I couldn't. We stood looking at each other, and then he snorted and shook his head and flung himself at me and I found myself flat on my back with the bully kneeling on my chest. Blood from his nose was dripping on to my face, so I turned my head to one side.

I knew what he was going to do. His favourite trick when he had somebody down was to grab a double handful of his victim's hair, just above the ears, and bang his head to the ground again and again. Kenneth Smith in Standard Two had to have stitches after Simcox did that to him. I bucked and writhed but it was no use—I couldn't shake him off, so I screwed up my eyes and prepared for the worst.

I suppose if I gave you three guesses, you wouldn't guess what happened next. There I was with my eyes

closed, waiting for torture to start, and suddenly Clive Simcox burst into tears. As I opened my eyes to look at him, he sort of slid off me on to the ground and lay with his hands over his face, rocking himself and sobbing.

I didn't know what to do. I sat up and looked at him and after a bit I said, 'What's up?'

'My dad,' he choked. 'He's dead.'

As I mentioned, Simcox senior worked at the button factory. How could he be dead?

'Dead?' I gasped. 'How?'

'Yesterday. The raid on the aerodrome.'

'But—your dad's in the factory. What was he doing on the aerodrome?'

'He wasn't on the aerodrome,' he sobbed. 'A stick of bombs fell short. One hit a house near the factory.'

'Oh, yes—my mum mentioned it, but . . . '

'The house collapsed, see? Most of the people got out but a little girl was trapped. It was Dad's lunch break. He crawled into the wreckage to get the kid, and the whole lot fell in on him.'

I understood then all right, but I still didn't know what to do so I laid a hand on his shoulder and said, 'He was a hero, your dad.'

I thought it might help, but it did the opposite. A fresh howl burst from him and he cried, 'I know, and I was ashamed of him because he wasn't in the Army like everybody else's dad. I haven't even talked to him for months, and now it's too late.'

Well. Most families had somebody to mourn in those days. People tried to help—meant to be kind—but in the end you just had to get through it. And you did get through it, but it changed you.

It changed Clive Simcox all right. The bullying stopped. He'd been acting tough to make up for his

dad not being in the Army, see? He thought kids were sneering behind his back and maybe they were, some of them. People can be very cruel—kids especially. Anyway they gave Simcox senior a medal, and quite right too. Clive had to go to Buckingham Palace and be presented. That bucked him up a bit, but it didn't cancel out the thing that haunted him. Fifty years have gone by since then and he still wishes he'd been nicer to his dad. He doesn't go on about it, but I know because we're best friends. You know—like Britain and Germany. Makes you wonder why we had to fight in the first place, doesn't it?

Dulce et Decorum est

Bent double, like old beggars under sacks,
Knock-kneed, coughing like hags, we cursed through
  sludge,
Till on the haunting flares we turned our backs.
And towards our distant rest began to trudge.
Men marched asleep. Many had lost their boots,
But limped on, blood-shod. All went lame, all
  blind;
Drunk with fatigue; deaf even to the hoots
Of gas-shells dropping softly behind.

Gas! Gas! Quick boys!—An ecstasy of fumbling,
Fitting the clumsy helmets just in time,
But someone still was yelling out and stumbling
And floundering like a man in fire or lime.—
Dim through the misty panes and thick green
  light,
As under a green sea, I saw him drowning.
In all my dreams, before my helpless sight,
He plunges at me, guttering, choking, drowning.

If in some smothering dreams, you too could pace
Behind the wagon that we flung him in,
And watch the white eyes writhing in his face,
His hanging face, like a devil's sick of sin;
If you could hear, at every jolt, the blood
Come gargling from the froth-corrupted lungs,
Obscene as cancer, bitter as the cud
Of vile, incurable sores on innocent tongues,—
My friend, you would not tell with such high
  zest
To children ardent for some desperate glory,
The old Lie: *Dulce et decorum est*
Pro patria mori.

Wilfred Owen

This powerful poem was written by a young officer in World War I, Wilfred Owen (1891–1918). In response to those at home in England who were telling soldiers how sweet and fitting it was to die for their country, he penned this bitter verse describing the horrors of war. He himself lost his life just a week before the war's end, at the age of 27.

from *Mother Earth*

CHINGIZ AITMATOV

Chingiz Aitmatov is a Kirgiz author writing in Russian. He wrote *Mother Earth* (*Materinskoye polye*) in 1963. It features a humble peasant woman, Tolgonai, who tells the story of her life in a wheatfield to Mother Earth. Much of her story is set in World War II, that terrible tragedy in which so many Soviet people died—including her husband Suvankul, and her three sons Kasym (and his wife Aliman), Maselbek, and Jainak. Now she is all alone, apart from her little grandson Zhanbolot. One day soon she will have to tell the little boy the whole story. But how?

Mother Earth, translated by James Riordan, appeared in English in 1989.

She was walking slowly along the path amid the stubble, wearing a light freshly-laundered dress, a dark quilted jacket, and a white headscarf. Nobody was about. Summer sounds had faded. No human voices drifting across the field, no lorries clouding the lanes,

no harvesters whirring in the distance, no flock of sheep yet brought to graze.

Beyond the grey highway, far, far away stretched the autumn steppe. Noiselessly above it drifted misty ridges of cloud. Noiselessly the breeze was stealing through the field, rippling the feather grass and dry corn stalks, silently departing for the river. There was a smell of grass dampened in the morning frosts. The earth was now resting after harvest. Soon it would be turning cold, the rains would come, the first snow would powder the soil and snowstorms would burst upon the plains. But for the moment all was still and quiet.

Do not disturb her. There she is now, stopping, gazing long about her through time-dimmed eyes.

'Good morning, field,' she says quietly.

'Good morning, Tolgonai. So you have come? A little older now. Quite grey. You carry a stick.'

'Yes, I'm growing old. Another year has passed; and for you, field, another harvest. It is remembrance day.'

'I know. I've been expecting you, Tolgonai. Not all history is to be found in books, not all history is in people's memories. But all history is within me. Your life, too, Tolganai, is within me, in my heart. I hear you, Tolgonai. Today is your day.'

That day we began reaping a new row of corn on the steep slope of the riverbank. The strip of land was too awkward for the harvester to turn, yet the ears were already dry—they always ripen faster along the edge of the field. Just as we had turned in single file and cut the corn, no more than two sheaves each, a horseman suddenly appeared on the other side. He had galloped out from behind the last houses beyond the river and, raising a trail of dust, was riding headlong through the

bushes and reeds as if someone was chasing him. His mount brought him down to the rocks along the bank. Yet unflinchingly he drove the horse straight over the rocks into the river.

We straightened up in amazement: what need was driving this man, why wasn't he making for the bridge a mile or so downriver? It was a young Russian lad. All the while he was urging his chestnut stallion into the water, and we all gasped: was he going to drown himself? You don't jest with the river at this time of year: at floodtide the waters would carry off a camel, let alone a horse, and not leave hair nor hide.

'Something must have happened, Mother,' Aliman cried as she broke into a run.

Her words pierced my heart.

'Someone must have fallen under the blade! Or got caught up in the drum. Quick!'

And all the reapers rushed after Aliman.

'Hold on, dear God, hold on,' I prayed, wringing my hands as I ran. Jumping over the ditch I missed my footing and went sprawling in the dust, quickly scrambled to my feet and ran on. Oh, how I ran through the wheatfield. I wanted to shout for them to wait, but I couldn't, I had lost my voice.

When I finally reached the combine, a crowd was milling about. I couldn't hear a word, couldn't make out a thing. Pushing through the crowd, yelling, 'Out of my way, let me pass,' I finally caught sight of Kasym and Aliman together beside the combine; I held out my trembling hands to my son like a blind woman. Kasym took a step forward and caught me.

'It's war, Mother.'

I heard his voice from far, far away.

I looked at him incredulously.

'War? Did you say war?'

'Yes, Mother, war,' he replied.

I still could not grasp the full meaning of the word.

'What do you mean war? What war?' I said, repeating the strange word; and then all at once I gasped in horror and quietly wept from the fright I had just had from this startling news.

The tears streamed down my face, as women, taking their cue from me, began to wail and moan.

'Quiet. Shut up!' a man's voice cut through the din.

Everyone fell silent together, as if half-expecting the fellow to say it was not so. But he said nothing. And no one else said anything. It became so quiet in the prairie that the water's booming roar could be clearly heard from the river. Someone sighed loudly and gave a shudder. It all went quiet again, expectant, though no one uttered a word. And once more the prairie became so still you could sense the heat, like a mosquito's shrill whine in your ear. And then, glancing at the people about him, Kasym muttered, half to himself. 'We'll have to hurry if we're to get the corn in before the snow comes.'

One winter's morning early I set out for the smithy. The blacksmith was reshoeing our draught horses. And I saw Usenbai flying along on his horse with a scrap of paper in his hand; he said it was an urgent telegram for me. I caught my breath. All I heard was the smith's hammer beating on the anvil, as if hitting me in the chest. I must have looked terrible.

'It's all right, Tolgonai,' he yelled. 'It's a telegram from Maselbek, from Novosibirsk. Come and get it, don't be afraid.'

And reaching down from the saddle, he handed me the paper.

'Go to the station at once,' he said. 'Your son will be passing through; he wants to see you, asks you to meet the train. I've told them to fix you up with a cart, with hay and oats for the horses. Don't just stand there, get going.'

A wave of joy swept over me. I flapped about, rushed around the forge not knowing what to do; finally the blacksmith chased me out.

'We'll cope by ourselves,' he said. 'Get off to the station fast, chief, otherwise you'll be late.'

Off home I ran. I still didn't fully understand what was going on. All I knew was that Maselbek had asked me to come to the station, that he wanted to see me. So there I was running down the street, hot from the frost, breaking out in a sweat. As I ran I was talking to myself like a mad thing, 'What does that mean, "asks me to meet the train"? Yes, yes, my son, I'd run a thousand miles to see you.'

A mother is always a mother. I didn't stop to think where he was heading.

Once home I hurriedly made some bits and pieces to eat, cooked some meat; Maselbek would certainly not be alone, he'd have his friends with him; let him treat them to some home cooking. I packed it all into a saddlebag and left for the station that very day with Aliman.

We reached the station towards evening. The moment the cart stopped, out Aliman jumped and ran to the track as if Maselbek were arriving at any moment. There was no one around. We stared in all directions and felt quite miserable, standing there like orphans, not knowing where to go or what to do. The wind rushed over the sleepers between the rails. A locomotive was crawling backwards and forwards, screeching and clanking, shunting trucks stuck fast with hoarfrost. The breeze whistled in the wires.

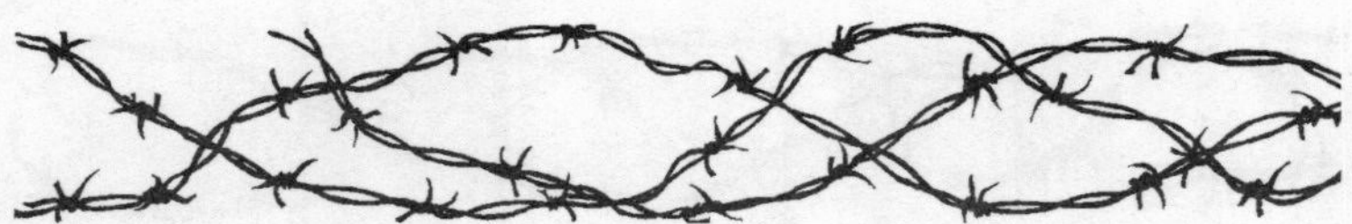

Troop trains came and went, but Maselbek wasn't on any of them. At midnight the ground began to shake again, we jumped up and dashed outside. From both directions at once we heard the shrill blasts of a train: two trains were approaching from different directions. We panicked, rushed this way and that, and found ourselves caught between the two tracks. With a deafening roar the trains came together and, without stopping, gathered speed and flashed through. The wheels rattled, the wind howled, enveloping us in a snowy whirlwind that tried to drag us under the wheels.

'Mother,' screamed Aliman and, gripping my arm, she pressed me against the lamppost, hugging me tight, not letting me go.

I peered into the windows as they flew by: what if I caught a glimpse of Maselbek, what if my son had been there and I'd not known? The rails groaned under the racing wheels and my heart echoed them in fear for my son. The train had flashed past in a cloud of snow while we stood pressed to the lamppost for a long while after.

We did not sit down until dawn, what with racing to and fro the length of the trains. Just before dawn as the blizzard momentarily ceased, yet another troop train was approaching from the west—but a very strange-looking one: the carriages were all charred, the roof was torn off, its doors were jagged and splintered. Not a living soul was on it. The vacant coaches were as silent as the grave; they smelt of smoke, hot iron, charred wood and paint.

Our acquaintance of the previous day, the man in the black sheepskin coat, came up, swinging a lamp.

To Aliman's whispered question about the train he replied, also in a whisper, 'It's been bombed.'

'Where are the carriages going?'

'For repair,' he answered just as reverently.

As I listened to the conversation I thought of those who had travelled in the carriages, those who had lost their lives amid smoke, screams and flames, those who had had arms and legs blown off, who had been deafened and blinded for life. Yet those bombs were a mere splinter of war. What was war itself like, then?

At that instant we heard the rumble of a train in the distance. It was coming from the east. Two loud blasts from the whistle echoed round the hollow.

The ground beneath our feet began to shake, the rails hummed, and two black engines with red wheels roared through the clouds of steam; they were pulling platforms with tarpaulin-covered tanks and guns guarded by soldiers in greatcoats, rifles at the ready. Soldiers flashed by in half-open doorways of heated goods vans and we caught a glimpse of faces, greatcoats and snatches of song, words, sounds of concertinas and balalaikas—vanload after vanload. We stood rooted to the spot. In the meantime some fellow with red and yellow signal flags came running over, shouting at us, 'Out of the way, out of the way. Get back, get back from the track!'

And he tried to shove us back.

Right at that moment we heard a shout, 'Mother-r-r! Alima-a-an!'

It was him! Maselbek! Oh my God, my God.

He was flying past so close, hanging out of a goods van, holding on to the door with one hand and waving his fur hat with the other, yelling, shouting farewell. All I remember is shrieking 'Maselbek!' And in that brief instant I saw him so plainly, so vividly: the wind was ruffling his hair, his coat tails were flapping like wings, and in his face and eyes were such joy and

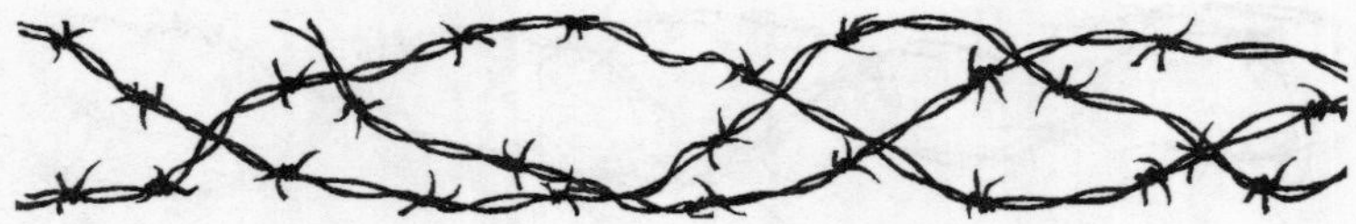

sorrow, regret and farewell. Not taking my eye off him for a second, I began running after the train. The last goods van rumbled by, but I kept running along the sleepers until I fell down. Oh, how I moaned and wept! There was my son leaving for the battlefield with me bidding him farewell, embracing a cold iron rail. The tapping of the wheels grew fainter and fainter and eventually died away.

Even now at times I can see that train and hear its wheels clanking.

Aliman came running up, tears streaming down her face; she crouched over me, vainly trying to pick me up, choking back her sobs, her hands shaking. At that moment a Russian woman from the signal box bustled up. She too cried, 'Mother, Mother!'

And she hugged and kissed me. The pair of them helped me to the trackside and, as we were leaving the station, Aliman handed me a soldier's hat.

'Here, Mother,' she said. 'Maselbek left it for you.'

Evidently he had thrown me his hat as I ran after the train. I travelled home in the cart holding the fur hat tightly, pressing it to my heart. It hangs on the wall to this day. Just a common grey soldier's hat with a little star. Sometimes I take it down and bury my face in it to try to bring back my son's smell.

'Tell me, dear earth, when did a mother suffer so just to catch a brief glimpse of her son?'

'I don't know, Tolgonai. The world has never known such a war as in your time.'

'Then may I be the last mother to await her son like that. Dear God, never again let anyone embrace iron rails and beat their head upon the sleepers.'

'When you returned home, I could tell from afar

you hadn't met your son. Your face was sallow and there were deep rings under your tortured eyes, like after a long illness.'

'Indeed, I would rather have been struck down with a fever.'

'My dear Tolgonai, your hair turned grey that year. How heavy and thick your plaits once were. You became silent then, withdrawn. You would come here in silence and leave, clenching your teeth. But I understood, I could tell by your eyes how it was getting harder with each visit.'

'Yes, Mother Earth, life can change a person so much. I wasn't the only one, there was not a single family, not a single person unaffected by the war. And when the black-edged papers arrived, what wailing and weeping there would be in two or three homes at once, and then my blood would boil and vengeance would dim my eyes, and sear my heart. I'm proud to have been the team chief at that time, partaking in my own and others' grief, sharing all misfortunes with people, their hunger and hardship. That's why I survived, withstood it for the sake of others; otherwise I would have gone under and the war would have trampled me into the dust. I realized then that there was only one way to win the war and that was to fight, to battle on, and to triumph. The alternative was death. That's why, my beloved field, I always came here on horseback, never disturbing you, greeting you silently and turning away in silence.

'Mother Earth, why don't the mountains crumble, why don't the lakes overflow when men such as Suvankul and Kasym are killed? They were both, father and son, great farmers. The world eternally relies on such people, they feed and nourish it, and in wartime protect it. They are the first to answer the call to arms.

If not for war, how much would Suvankul and Kasym have accomplished? How many more people would have benefited from the fruits of their labour? How many more fields would have been sown? How much more wheat would have been harvested? And they themselves, rewarded a hundred-fold by the labours of their fellow men, would have known so much happiness.

'Tell me, Mother Earth, speak truly: can people live without war?'

'You pose a difficult question, Tolgonai. There have been nations that vanished without trace in wars; there have been cities consumed by fire and buried under the ashes; there have been barren centuries when I yearned for human company. And each time people went to war I told them, "Stop, spill no blood!" I say it again now: "You people beyond the mountains and the seas, you people of the world, what is it you want—the earth? Here I am—take me. I am the same for all of you, and you are all equal in my eyes. I have no need of your quarrels, I need your friendship, your labour. Cast a single grain into a furrow and I'll give you a hundred back. Stick a twig in me and I'll grow you a tree. Plant a garden and I'll shower you with fruit. Breed your cattle and I'll be your grass. Build homes and I'll be your walls. Reproduce and multiply and I shall be a splendid abode for you all. I am endless, I am infinite, I am deep and tall, there's more than enough for everyone."

'And you, Tolgonai, you ask if people can live without war. But that depends on you human beings, not me, upon your will and common sense.'

'You're right, dear earth, war does kill your very best labourers, your best craftsmen. That's a terrible crime, my whole being revolts against it. People can, people must bar the way to war.'

'Do you think I don't suffer from war? I suffer cruelly. I miss the farmer's hands. I am forever mourning for my children, tillers of the soil, I shall forever miss Suvankul, Kasym, Jainak and all the fallen heroes. Whenever I'm left untilled, whenever the harvests remain unreaped and the corn unthreshed, I call out to them: "Where are you now, my tillers? Where are you now, my sowers? Arise, my children, my toilers. Come to my aid, I am choking, I am dying."

'If only Suvankul would then appear hoe in hand; if only Kasym would bring his combine; if only Jainak would come in his cart. But they do not hear.'

'Thank you, earth, for all that you have said. So you miss them too, as I do. You weep for them too, as I do. Thank you.'

'Oh my cherished field, you are now at rest after harvest. No human voices to be heard, no lorries to raise a trail of dust, no combines to be seen, no flocks of sheep have come yet to graze in the stubble. You have given people the fruits of the earth and can now lie back like a woman after birth.

'You may rest until autumn ploughing. There are only the two of us, you and I, no one else. You know the story of my life. Today is remembrance day. Today I honour the memory of Suvankul, Kasym, Maselbek, Jainak, and Aliman. I shall remember them as long as I live. The time will come when I'll tell Zhanbolot everything. If he has been blessed with a mind and a heart he will understand. But what about others? All the other people living in the world? I have something to say to them. How can I reach their hearts?

'Hey, sun, shining up in the sky, you encircle the globe, you tell them.

'Hey, raincloud, fall upon the world in a bright shower and tell them in each raindrop.

'Earth, Mother-Provider, you support us all upon your bosom, you nourish people in every corner of the earth, you tell them. Dear earth, you tell people.'

'No, Tolgonai, you tell them. You are a human being. You are higher than us all, you are wiser than us all, you are a human being. You tell them.'

'Are you going, Tolgonai?'

'Yes. If I'm still alive I'll be back. Farewell, Mother Earth.'

APO 96225

A young man once went off to war
in a far country.
When he had time, he wrote home and
said, 'Sure rains here a lot.'

But his mother, reading between the lines,
wrote, 'We're quite concerned. Tell us
what it's really like.'

And the young man responded, 'Wow, you ought
to see the funny monkeys!'

To which the mother replied, 'Don't
hold back, how is it?'

And the young man wrote, 'The sunsets here
are spectacular.'

In her next letter the mother
wrote, 'Son, we want you to tell us
everything.'

So the next time he wrote,
'Today I killed a man.
Yesterday I helped drop napalm on women and
children. Tomorrow we are going to use
gas.'

And the father wrote, 'Please don't
write such depressing letters. You're upsetting
your mother.'

So, after a while, the young man wrote, 'Sure rains a
lot here . . . '

Larry Rottman

from *The War Orphan*

RACHEL ANDERSON

Rachel Anderson's story, published in 1984, is a powerful tale about the war in Vietnam, as seen through the eyes of a child living in a riverside village. The village is invaded by a group of American soldiers searching for what they call the Viet Cong (VC), also known as the People's Army. At the time, Vietnam is divided into the North, controlled by the communists, and the South, occupied by the US Army.

Our village lay inside a small loop of the river, and was rich, fertile land. The soil was dark-red so that, during the dry season, red dust clung to the grass and the leaves, and the air was close and still. But after the rainy season, everything grew new and green.

Beside the river we had rice paddies, and on the higher land we had fruit orchards and vegetable plots where we grew mangoes, bread-fruit, grapefruit, and pineapples. Beyond the village we had plantations of bananas, and groves of bamboo. And beyond the bamboo came the forest.

Some families kept water-buffalo who did the work for them. In my family, we had a cow for milk, some hens, and a goat. We harvested enough rice and vegetables for our family and the rest my mother sent downriver to market in the city. But we had to keep some rice back to pay our taxes to the men from the North, and a few vegetables to give as presents to the men from the South.

The men from the South usually came with the foreigners. The foreigners looked different from us. Their skin was pale and their forearms hairy. We children used to call them the round-eyes, though their eyes weren't really round.

Then one day the helicopters came. We watched them circle, then bump down, one after another in rapid succession, on to our vegetable gardens. The men jumped out and ran, bent double as though themselves afraid of being fired on, over melons, beans, celery, trampling with their boots on whatever produce hadn't already been destroyed by shells.

They were disciplined and determined. There were none of the Government puppet troops in the first wave. They were all the foreign round-eyes. They were fanning out, to encircle our village.

'We must go in,' said my mother, and she hurried us inside.

But my grandmother was in a trance, dazed by three nights in the shelter. My mother sat her down gently on the stool and gave her the baby to hold while she saw to the clearing up.

The room was suddenly darkened by a huge man, higher than the door lintel, blocking out the light. He was so tall that he had to stoop to stand in the doorway, and even then the top of his helmet was lost in the grass-thatch.

'Where's your husband, lady?' he shouted.

His skin was as dark as ripe figs, his nostrils wide open like a boar's snout, his eyes bulbous and red-rimmed. He held an automatic low at his hip and pointed it first at my grandmother with the baby, then at my mother.

My mother snatched the baby back from my grandmother and held it to her tightly. The huge dark man instinctively twitched his gun back at her. He was very frightened.

'Your husband! Where is he?'

He didn't see me. I was in the folds of my father's jacket hanging on a peg. But as I flattened myself more against the wall I knocked an earthenware dish down from the shelf. It clattered to the floor.

The jumpy black man shot over our heads into the roof and one of the hens, roosting in the thatch, caught the hail of fire and flopped down to the ground, dead but still squarking. The man swung round and fired into the garden, then swung back to us, and took a step hesitantly into the house, gesturing with his gun.

'Where's your husband?' he shouted.

She didn't understand. He shouted it again. I knew what he was saying. The People's Army had told us not to spoil our mother tongue with foreign languages, but how could I help it if I understood everything they said?

She stared at him, not insolent, not stupid, just stared.

Without moving further into the room, he looked carefully round. It was quite small. There was nowhere for a man to be hiding. My parents' cane bed on one side, the baby's basket, my bedroll. Our possessions hanging from pegs on the walls. We cook in another

room with open sides. The soldier saw the wicker basket full of our clothes, all dusted in red.

He began to poke into it with the point of his gun.

'Clothes!' my mother said. But he didn't understand her any more than she understood him. Although I could understand both, I didn't know how to explain his words to her.

She took out the dusty red garments, one by one, and the soldier watched carefully, then nodded.

'OK, I get the message. That's your laundry bin. Now where's your husband?'

My mother remained standing where she was. He had the gun. She had the baby. I could see her growing angry, but outwardly she looked calm. She was very beautiful. 'I don't understand why you round-eyes keep on coming here,' she said quietly. 'Why can't you go away? You know, we're fed up with you round here.'

'All I have to know,' the black man yelled, 'is where is your husband?'

'You drop messages on us, you bomb the paddies,' my mother went on grumbling. 'You kill our livestock. What else do you want?'

The soldier seemed to despair of getting through to her.

He called out to another soldier who was searching through the hen-coops.

'What do I do with her?'

'Any weapons? She look suspect?'

'No, just a very pretty stack of woman, with an old crone, and a couple of kids.'

'Leave her.'

'OK, lady, you stay right here.' He turned and went away.

A minute later he was back with three others.

'You numbskull! You don't send them back into their homes. You round them up.'

So we were ordered out of the house, two soldiers behind us, one at the side, the leader shouting at them, telling them what to do. They all did a lot of shouting. We were silent.

'Your job's to keep anyone from escaping, right? Block off that path. No way through. If it's just a bunch of women and kids wandering about and don't know what's happening, don't fire. Just bring them in as best you can. But otherwise, you got to take them under fire. Anything that moves out there, that's VC. Got it?'

They used the loudspeakers attached to the first helicopter, to warn us we must move quickly to the centre of the village, otherwise we'd be shot as VC suspects.

I didn't know what VC was.

'It's their term,' said my mother. 'It means nothing to us. There's no VC, so none of us can be VC.'

But it did mean something to them. It was their word for any person who was with the People's Army or who knew anything about the People's Army, who had ever done anything for the People's Army. In their language, a VC suspect was any person who owned a pair of shoes, any person who owned a shirt with buttons, any person not carrying an Identification Card, any person who didn't wear a straw sunhat.

We were led, or shoved, or driven like a herd of buffaloes towards the school-hut.

'You have no father,' my mother said as we hurried along. 'If anybody questions you, remember he went away a long time ago. No father. Don't forget.'

My grandmother shuffled and muttered irritably.

But some of the little children went skipping along as though expecting a festival with pink drinks.

I knew something terrible was going to happen, worse than being in an air-raid for three days. Everything was going to change. We should turn and run while we had the chance, and hide in the green. But my mother didn't understand. She didn't hear the things the foreign soldiers said to one another. Only I understood and it was too difficult to explain. I only knew that, somehow, I had allowed the melodious purity of the mother tongue to be infiltrated by the language of the colonialist aggressors.

The soldiers had seemed so big and menacing when they streamed out of their helicopters. Now, closer to, they were young and jittery, and uncertain what they were to do. They were rough with us.

'What we gonna do with all these people?'

'Interrogation first. In the school house.'

'What after?'

'Resettlement. A good temporary camp.'

'Prisoner of war? But they aren't POWs. We just taken them out of their homes. They're civilians.'

'Hostile civilians. We've orders to clear this village, spring-cleaning. While we're doing that, they'll be safer in camp.'

'It doesn't seem right, somehow, moving them out when they've not done anything.'

'They'll be quite happy there. All amenities.'

We were assembled in the shade of the school house, everybody of the village who could be found. Then, we saw a solitary figure moving slowly away down the main street. It was old Giau Huc, on his bicycle, pedalling towards his vegetable garden, his straw hat tipped to the back of his head, his hoe and basket strapped to his bicycle carrier. He was deaf from an

explosion. He was also obstinate, and a bit stupid. He couldn't hear the loudspeakers. All the villagers' eyes were on him. One of the soldiers spotted him. He shouted after him. Giau Huc couldn't hear the shout. He pedalled on. We watched the distant figure, his round, yellow hat bright against the dark trees, and we all knew what was going to happen and we were unable to do anything about it. I seemed to see it all happen long before it really did, the slow flying fall of Giau Huc, gracefully sideways, with the sound coming after.

The soldier called after him again.

'Git back here! Do you hear me! Git on back here with the others! That's orders!'

Another soldier, very young, with a red face, and pale hair, raised his weapon.

Giau Huc's pedalling feet went on, round and round.

The young soldier fired, and a moment later, there were more bursts of machine-gun fire from another group of soldiers who'd also seen Giau Huc going the wrong way. Giau Huc seemed to move up in the air as though flying, in a slow spray of dust and movement, away above his bike, and then gently sideways and down into the rainwater ditch beside the path.

The young red-faced soldier ran cautiously towards the body, half crouching, as though afraid it might get up and fire back. When he saw there was no movement, he straightened up and stared at it for several moments as his friends gathered round.

'He's dead. Yep,' one of them said.

'That's a VC for you,' said another. 'He's a VC all right.'

'That's what they wear, them black pyjamas. That's their uniform, ain't it? He wouldn't wear that if he was a genuine farmer. It wouldn't make sense, on account

of black absorbs heat. It's a hot country, you don't wear black clothing out in the meadow, get too damned hot.'

'No, that can't be right, sir. That's no uniform. They all wear them black pyjamas, and the white shirt. All the people. Haven't you seen them back in town, all wearing that?'

'Sure they all wear it. They're all VC. Didn't you hear the captain telling us at the briefing? Solid VC country here, as long as anyone can remember, that's what he said. And look at his feet.'

Giau Huc had bare feet, brown.

'See! All muddy from burrowing down them holes they dig everywhere for living in. They're more like coneys than humans.'

'I don't think he was no VC. He don't have no weapon.'

The hoe lay on the ground beside Giau Huc. One of the soldiers kicked it with his toe-cap. 'What's that then, if it isn't a weapon? Of course he was VC. You saw him, moving away when he was told to stop. If he'd stopped when we told him to stop, he wouldn't have got shot, would he?'

'That's right.'

'Lieutenant told us we were to shoot if they move. But no women and kids.'

The red-faced man who'd fired the first shot at Giau Huc, bent over and peered closely into Giau Huc's face.

'I shot him!' he said. It was the first thing he'd said. 'That's the first time I ever killed anybody before!' He seemed surprised but not upset.

One of them had a black camera on a strap round his neck and he began to take photographs of the body.

A few of the soldiers tried to be playful and friendly.

They offered candybars to the smaller children, they tried to smile and chat to the girls. With elaborate gestures, they tried to find out their names, and explain their own. But we'd all seen Giau Huc shot. These men were as unlike human beings as the helicopters they had arrived in. They were like flying snakes, dangerous and unreliable.

They were larger than us, and armed and hairy. There was nothing to be done except obey their orders but not communicate. People's faces were closing off. They might have been dreaming with their eyes open, like the dead. Even the little children soon copied the mood of their parents, and sat still and silent.

The questioning went on all morning. It was hot and sultry. The sun rose higher and the air became drier.

Several long rattles of machine-gun fire sounded across the village near where Giau Huc had fallen. A man was firing random bursts into an outhouse. It was the same one who'd shot Giau Huc. Another soldier shouted angrily at him.

'Come back here! Stop that fooling around!'

But the red-faced boy went on shooting into the outhouse and into the yard beside it and into the trees until his target, a buffalo tethered to a post in a yard, finally sank to its knees, and rolled over on to its side with a groan.

'You're not to kill buffalo!'

The soldier-boy ambled back to the school house, grinning.

'What was he doing?'

'He says he doesn't remember what he was doing.'

'Does he pay taxes?'

'Yes. The men from the North come and collect two piastres a month.'

'What's his job?'

'He says he's a farmer.'

'Let's see his hands. Show me. He's no farmer! His palms are smooth, not hard and calloused. Ask him what he does.'

'He says he's been repairing bicycles for other people.'

'Why did he say he was a farmer then?'

'He says, he used to be a farmer, until Ben Rach was evacuated and then he came to live here with these people. He's been helping.'

'How has he been helping?'

'With the harvest, he says. But now he repairs bicycles.'

The questioning was less casual than the time before when they questioned my father. They sorted us into groups. The older boys and men were put on one side of the schoolyard, the women and children the other. I was with the women and children.

Each person was led, one by one, into a brown tent, while the rest stayed outside, sitting in the shade, watched over by the soldiers. Nobody talked. Nobody moved, they just listened to the endless murmuring of the interrogators' voices inside the tent.

My mother, with the baby resting on one arm, sat perfectly still, straight-backed, not looking at anybody, only staring ahead, her smooth face a blank. She moved only once, to nurse my sister.

At last, it was her turn. I got up to go with her.

'Not you, Sonny Jim,' said the soldier, and pushed me back from the open tent flap. I was afraid of what would happen to her in there, but instead of looking

frightened, she merely looked annoyed and glared angrily at the soldier who led her in. I sat down outside the tent and strained hard to hear.

The questioning was done by an American captain, with a Government soldier as interpreter.

'Has she ever seen VC?' said the captain. He spoke in a loud, flat voice.

'Have you ever seen VC?' said the interpreter. His voice was softer and quieter, rising and falling. My mother's voice was the quietest of all so that I could hardly hear.

'Yes, sometimes. Everybody knows they're about. But nobody knows who they are.'

'Yes, she says sometimes, of course,' said the interpreter.

'Where does she see them?'

'Where do you see them?'

'Out walking in the fields, many weeks ago,' said my mother.

'Where were they going?'

'She says she doesn't know. It's not her business to know about things like that. She says she lives in the village and looks after her old mother and her children. She says she doesn't go following strangers into the forest.'

'What were the VC doing in the fields?'

'How should I know?'

'She says she doesn't know. It's not her business.'

'Where's her husband?'

'Where's your husband?'

Perhaps the foreign captain should have asked different questions. Have you seen your husband lately? What were you doing last week at dawn before it was light? Why did you take a small bowl of rice and a parcel of cooked vegetables wrapped up in leaves into

the forest? Why did you walk quietly without a lamp, and leave your baby behind in the house?

But he didn't ask questions like that. He asked, with boredom, the same questions he asked everybody. And she gave the same answers.

'She says she doesn't know. He went away a long time ago, and it's been very hard. He might be dead for all she knows. There's been bombing. Mi Hung was flattened by raids. All the people had to come here to their village.'

'Is her husband VC?'

'She says, No, he isn't. She says she doesn't think anybody in this village is.'

'Well *somebody* must be!' said the captain. 'What's going on in this place? Every peasant we question has never known anybody who's VC, has never seen any VC close up. Don't they know there's a war going on all round them? How can we fight a war if we never make contact with an enemy? When we don't even know who the enemy is, let alone where?'

Instead of waiting for the next question my mother began to complain in a high, whining voice about what had happened in our village that morning.

'One of your soldiers, a great dark man, shot one of my hens roosting in the roof,' she said to the interpreter. 'Go on, tell him,' said my mother. 'You have to repeat what I say.'

'She says that this morning a soldier from your army shot one of her hens.'

'A good laying hen,' added my mother.

'A good layer,' said the interpreter.

'Who's going to pay for my hen?'

'Listen, woman, oh, tell her, we're fighting a war here. We're trying to liberate her country, not playing farmers. What's one hen compared to the loss of 12,000

young men? No, don't say that. She won't understand what I mean.'

My mother began to describe all the special things about the hen.

'Will you tell her to kindly answer the questions as they're put to her,' snapped the captain. 'Tell her she'll get compensation if she applies to the right source. God almighty, one laying hen! But she's quite right though. We've got to play down this shooting at the peasants' livestock, or we'll have HQ down on us like a ton of bricks. How do we expect these villagers to trust us if the troops go round letting fire at everything that moves? And as for that buffalo this morning, that'll cost us a few bucks. What's a buffalo worth these days?'

'Ten dollars, sir, or four hundred piastres. But it belonged to the VC suspect Private Armstrong shot on the bicycle. So maybe it won't cost us anything.'

My mother seemed to have decided she had answered enough questions. She went on and on about our cow. How the noise of the air raid would almost certainly dry up its milk. Then what would we do? How, moreover, could she answer questions in the middle of the afternoon, when she couldn't remember a thing because bombs were falling so loudly for the past three days. And if one hen could be shot while she was right there in her house, what might happen when she was not at home? Why wasn't she allowed to bring the rest of her livestock into the schoolyard with her, to keep it safe? By the time she returned home, she might find the whole lot had been shot at by the soldiers.

The interpreter, struggling to interpret my mother's quiet but unceasing complaints, said to the officer, 'This woman is very angry, sir. And very worried about her animals.'

The officer scratched his head. 'All right, let her go. Bring in the next.'

My mother came out of the tent, her back straight, her head up. She hitched the baby on to her hip and walked serenely, gracefully back to her place in the yard. She did not look into the eyes of anybody, not even me. But though her face was empty, I felt sure I could see a glow of triumph behind the sullen stare.

The soldiers made a pile of the things they'd found in a cache in the forest, and displayed them in front of us as evidence of the village's collective guilt. There were some rifles and grenades, some tin canteens, and several store-tins of rice.

'But that old man wasn't carrying a weapon, was he? We were told only shoot if they're carrying weapons. That's how you know they're the enemy.'

'Well OK. So some people without weapons get killed. So what are we supposed to do about it? We spot a guy out there in black pyjamas. What do we do? Wait for him to pull his AK-4 on us? I tell you I'm not. I'm going to get through this alive and then get on home. You're just a crispy critter, aren't you? That's because you're new out here. How long since you been here? One week? Two weeks? This the first time you been in an action situation?'

'Yes.'

'This the first time you seen men greased?'

'Yes.'

'You'll get to understand how it is out here in a while. Listen, son, how old are you?'

'Eighteen last week, sir. They made me stay on board till my birthday.'

'If you don't like fighting, you shoulda joined the Peace Corps. But if you want to survive, if you want to get on home and see your mom and pop, and if you

want to eat blueberry pie again, momma's own filling, you are gonna have to learn fast. Be sharp. On guard. Or else, as soon as you think you're safe, zap, some gook's gonna get you first. In combat, you don't get to have no second chances. OK?'

'Yes.'

'So maybe I'm wrong, and that poor old boy we got this morning was innocent. Maybe he was just an old granpappy. And maybe again he was not. Sometimes they throw their weapons into the bushes, far away, just as they hear you coming. You go and look at the body, and fifty yards away there's an automatic lying in the bushes. You can't always tell from a long way off if they're carrying a weapon, and you don't want to get too close to find out. Not if you want to get on home and enjoy a nice white Christmas next year.'

Some people came out of the interrogation tent with their arms tied behind their backs with twine, and a brown label on a string hanging round their necks. They weren't led back to their place, in the yard, but were taken over to the far corner.

A boy called Van Lan Long who was only three years older than me, was led out like that, with his arms tightly bound behind him, just above the elbow. He was barefoot and wearing only cotton shorts. The top of his head came up as far as the guard's ammunition belt.

'You mean this little kid's suspect?' one of the soldiers said.

'This kid, as you call him, has probably been gun-running for five years. A ten year old comes up, takes your candy, and next minute, wham, he drops his grenade! This innocent boy probably caused the death of a good many of your best buddies just like that.

Anyhow, these gooks always look younger than they are. They're a stunted race.'

Van Lan Long was pushed roughly towards the far corner. As he stumbled past, I saw the brown card label they'd put round his neck. 'Captive Card', it said, printed in our language and theirs, and underneath there were spaces to put the person's name and age and work. They'd filled in his name but left the rest empty.

Altogether, they selected twenty people as captives, including our village headman, and they sat them in two rows, squatting, their hands behind their backs, with a guard at each end of each row. We tried not to look directly at them. They were all people we knew, and they didn't look across at our side of the yard. Even wives didn't look at husbands, or mothers at sons.

A large helicopter, bigger than the ones the army had come in, landed bumpily in the road outside the school. It had two sets of whirling blades, one at each end, which blasted up red dust into our faces. The guards hid their faces in their arms against the swirling dust, and so did we. But the captives, with their arms tied, could only close their eyes and let the hot dust blow at them.

The back end of the helicopter was lowered, to form a bridge leading up into the dark opening of the inside. The captives were ordered, with gestures, to crouch low to avoid being chopped up by the whirling blades, and to run towards the opening.

They ran in single file, up the gangway and into the darkness, with their brown labels flapping in the wind.

The gang-plank was drawn up so that we couldn't see them any more. The helicopter took off with more roaring and wind. Seventeen men and three boys from our village were lifted up, soaring above our heads into the sky, and disappeared away over the trees.

What Were They Like?

1) Did the people of Vietnam
   use lanterns of stone?
2) Did they hold ceremonies
   to reverence the opening of buds?
3) Were they inclined to quiet laughter?
4) Did they use bone and ivory,
   jade and silver, for ornament?
5) Had they an epic poem?
6) Did they distinguish between speech and singing?

1) Sir, their light hearts turned to stone.
   It is not remembered whether in gardens
   stone lanterns illumined pleasant ways.
2) Perhaps they gathered once to delight in blossom,
   but after the children were killed
   there were no more buds.
3) Sir, laughter is bitter to the burned mouth.
4) A dream ago, perhaps. Ornament is for joy.
   All the bones were charred.
5) It is not remembered. Remember,
   most were peasants; their life
   was in rice and bamboo.
   When peaceful clouds were reflected in the paddies
   and the water buffalo stepped surely along terraces,
   maybe fathers told their sons old tales.
   When bombs smashed those mirrors
   there was time only to scream.
6) There is an echo yet
   of their speech which was like a song.
   It was reported their singing resembled
   the flight of moths in moonlight.
   Who can say? It is silent now.

Denise Levertov

Aftermath

Have you forgotten yet? . . .
For the world's events have rumbled on since those gagged days,
Like traffic checked awhile at the crossing of city-ways:
And the haunted gap in your mind has filled with thoughts that flow
Like clouds in the lit heaven of life; and you're a man reprieved to go,
Taking your peaceful share of Time, with joy to spare.
But the past is just the same—and War's a bloody game . . .
Have you forgotten yet? . . .
Look down, and swear by the slain of the war that you'll never forget.

Do you remember the dark months you held the sector at Mametz—
The nights you watched and wired and dug and piled sandbags on parapets?
Do you remember the rats; and the stench
Of corpses rotting in front of the front-line trench—
And dawn coming, dirty-white, and chill with a hopeless rain?
Do you ever stop and ask, 'Is it all going to happen again?'

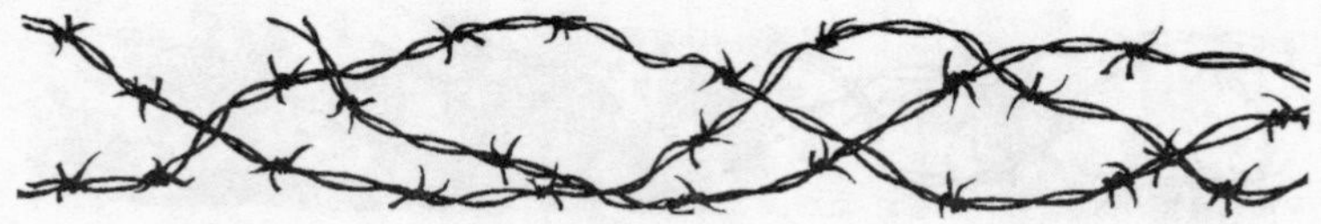

Do you remember that hour of din before the attack—
And the anger, the blind compassion that seized and
  shook you then
As you peered at the doomed and haggard faces of
  your men?
Do you remember the stretcher-cases lurching back
With dying eyes and lolling heads—those ashen-grey
Masks of the lads who once were keen and kind and
  gay?

Have you forgotten yet? . . .
Look up, and swear by the green of the spring that you'll
  never forget.

Siegfried Sassoon

Siegfried Sassoon (1886–1967) was another of the 'war poets' who fought in World War I and wrote a bitter condemnation of the horrors of war. He attempted to desert and, in 1917, his protest against the war was read out in the House of Commons. Badly wounded in July 1918, he returned to England where he wrote many fine poems against war.

Chronology of Major Twentieth-Century Wars

First World War

28 June 1914 Archduke Franz Ferdinand of Austria is assassinated by Serbians in Bosnia
23 July 1914 Austria, supported by Germany, declares war on Serbia. Russia defends Serbia, so Austria and Germany declare war on Russia, an ally of France which also joins the war
4 August 1914 When Germany invades Belgium (to reach France), Britain joins the Allies (France and Russia)
4 April 1917 USA joins the Allies
11 November 1918 The Great War ends after 1,561 days with Germany's defeat

TOTAL DEAD: About ten million
WOUNDED or MISSING: About twenty million

Second World War

30 January 1933 Adolf Hitler and his Nazi Party come to power in Germany
1 April 1933 First law passed against the half million Jews living in Germany
15 March 1939 German troops march into Czechoslovakia
1 September 1939 Germany declares war on Poland
3 September 1939 The Allies (France, Britain) declare war on Germany
22 June 1941 Hitler attacks the Soviet Union, which joins the war
14 October 1941 The large-scale deportation of Jews to concentration camps begins

7 December 1941 Germany's ally Japan attacks the US fleet in Pearl Harbour, drawing America into the war
8 May 1945 Germany surrenders. The War ends after 2,228 days

TOTAL DEAD: Over eighty million, including forty million Soviet people, thirteen million Chinese, nine million Poles, and six million Jews
WOUNDED or MISSING: Over 150 million

Vietnam War

1954 After eight years of fighting between French (colonial) forces and communist partisans in the north, the defeated French leave and the country is divided into north and south
early 1960s North Vietnam sends communist troops (the Viet Cong) into the south to overthrow its pro-Western government. The USA responds by sending in 2,000 'military advisers'
1965 onwards More and more US (and Australian) troops are sent, peaking at about a million in 1969
1969–73 US planes bomb neutral Laos and Cambodia
1973 USA withdraws after world-wide protests. Almost at once communist troops occupy the whole country

TOTAL DEAD: About three million, including one million North Vietnamese soldiers, one million civilians, 500,000 Cambodians and Laotians, and 56,555 US soldiers
DAMAGE: The USA used napalm and other mass-destruction bombs to destroy 50 per cent of the country's forest and 20 per cent of its agricultural land

Acknowledgements

Chingiz Aitmatov: 'Mother Earth' from *Mother Earth*, translated by James Riordan (Faber, 1989), originally published in the Kirgiz language as 'Materinskoye Polye', 1963, copyright © 1963, 1989 by Chingiz Aitmatov, reprinted by permission of Liepman AG on behalf of Chingiz Aitmatov.

Rachel Anderson: extract from *The War Orphan* (OUP, 1984), reprinted by permission of Oxford University Press.

Bertolt Brecht: 'To Posterity' translated by Michael Hamburger from *German Poetry 1910–1975* edited by Michael Hamburger (Carcanet Press, 1977), reprinted by permission of Michael Hamburger.

Anne Frank: extract from *The Diary of a Young Girl: The Definitive Edition* edited by Otto H. Frank and Mirjam Pressler, translated by Susan Massoty (Viking, 1997), copyright © The Anne Frank-Fonds, Basle, Switzerland, 1991, English translation copyright © Doubleday, a division of Bantam Doubleday Dell Publishing Group Inc., 1995, reprinted by permission of Penguin Books Ltd and Doubleday, a division of Random House, Inc.

Anne Holm: extract from *I Am David* (Methuen, 1965), English translation copyright © 1965 Methuen & Co. Ltd, first published in Danish as *David* (Gyldendal, Copenhagen, 1963), reprinted by permission of the publisher, Egmont Children's Books Ltd, London.

Denise Levertov: 'What Were They Like' from *Selected Poems* (Bloodaxe Books), reprinted by permission of Laurence Pollinger Ltd, also from *Poems 1960–1967*, copyright © 1966 Denise Levertov, reprinted by permission of New Directions Publishing Corporation.

A. A. Milne: 'OBE' from *The Sunny Side*, copyright 1921 by A. A. Milne, reprinted by permission of Curtis Brown Ltd, London.

Michael Morpurgo: extract from *War Horse* (Kaye & Ward, 1982), copyright © Michael Morpurgo 1982, reprinted by permission of the publisher, Egmont Children's Books Ltd, London.

E. M. Remarque: extract from *All Quiet on the Western Front* (Jonathan Cape), English translation copyright © Jonathan Cape 1994, reprinted by permission of The Random House Group Ltd.

Hans Peter Richter: extract from *Friedrich* (Puffin, 1987) translated from the German by Edite Kroll, copyright © Sebaldus-Verlag GmbH Nurnberg, 1961, copyright © Holt, Rinehart and Winston, Inc., 1970, reprinted by permission of Penguin Books Ltd.

Siegfried Sassoon: 'Aftermath' from *Collected Poems of Siegfried Sassoon*, copyright 1918, 1920 by E. P. Dutton, copyright © 1936, 1946, 1947, 1948 by Siegfried Sassoon, reprinted by permission of Barbara Levy Literary Agency and Viking Penguin, a division of Penguin Putnam Inc.

Ian Serraillier: extract from *The Silver Sword* (Jonathan Cape, 1956) reprinted by permission of Anne Serraillier.

Franz Baermann Steiner: '8th May 1945' translated by Michael Hamburger from *German Poetry 1910–1975* edited by Michael Hamburger (Carcanet Press, 1977), reprinted by permission of Michael Hamburger.

Robert Swindells: extract from *Hurricane Summer* (Mammoth, an imprint of Egmont Children's Books Ltd, 1977), copyright © Robert Swindells 1977, reprinted by permission of the publisher.

Ruth Tomalin: 'Ladybird, Ladybird' from *Threnody for Dormice* (Fortune Press, 1947), reprinted by permission of the author.

Georg Trakl: 'At the Eastern Front' translated by Michael Hamburger from *German Poetry 1910–1975* edited by Michael Hamburger (Carcanet Press, 1977), reprinted by permission of Michael Hamburger.

Robert Westall: extract from *A Time of Fire* (Pan Macmillan, 1994), copyright © 1994 Robert Westall, reprinted by permission of Macmillan Publishers Ltd.

Despite every effort to trace and contact copyright holders prior to publication, this has not always been possible in a few cases. If notified, the publisher will be pleased to rectify any errors or omissions at the earliest opportunity.